CINDERELLA AND OTHER STORIES

Charles Perrault

Translated by A. E. Johnson

COLLINS
CLASSICS

William Collins

An imprint of HarperCollins*Publishers*
1 London Bridge Street
London SE1 9GF

WilliamCollinsBooks.com

This William Collins paperback edition
published in Great Britain in 2015

3

A catalogue record for this book
is available from the British Library

ISBN 978-0-00-814745-7

Printed and bound in Great Britain by
CPI Group (UK) Ltd, Croydon CR0 4YY

MIX
Paper | Supporting
responsible forestry
FSC™ C007454
FSC
www.fsc.org

This book contains FSC™ certified paper and other controlled
sources to ensure responsible forest management.

For more information visit: www.harpercollins.co.uk/green

Life & Times section © HarperCollins*Publishers* Ltd
Silvia Crompton asserts her moral rights as author of the Life & Times section
Classic Literature: Words and Phrases adapted from
Collins English Dictionary

Typesetting in Kalix by Palimpsest Book Production Limited,
Falkirk, Stirlingshire

History of Collins

In 1819, millworker William Collins from Glasgow, Scotland, set up a company for printing and publishing pamphlets, sermons, hymn books, and prayer books. That company was Collins and was to mark the birth of HarperCollins Publishers as we know it today. The long tradition of Collins dictionary publishing can be traced back to the first dictionary William published in 1824, *Greek and English Lexicon*. Indeed, from 1840 onwards, he began to produce illustrated dictionaries and even obtained a licence to print and publish the Bible.

Soon after, William published the first Collins novel, *Ready Reckoner*; however, it was the time of the Long Depression, where harvests were poor, prices were high, potato crops had failed, and violence was erupting in Europe. As a result, many factories across the country were forced to close down and William chose to retire in 1846, partly due to the hardships he was facing.

Aged 30, William's son, William II, took over the business. A keen humanitarian with a warm heart and a generous spirit, William II was truly 'Victorian' in his outlook. He introduced new, up-to-date steam presses and published affordable editions of Shakespeare's works and *The Pilgrim's Progress*, making them available to the masses for the first time. A new demand for educational books meant that success came with the publication of travel books, scientific books, encyclopedias, and dictionaries. This demand to be educated led to the later publication of atlases, and Collins also held the monopoly on scripture writing at the time.

In the 1860s Collins began to expand and diversify

and the idea of 'books for the millions' was developed. Affordable editions of classical literature were published, and in 1903 Collins introduced 10 titles in their Collins Handy Illustrated Pocket Novels. These proved so popular that a few years later this had increased to an output of 50 volumes, selling nearly half a million in their year of publication. In the same year, The Everyman's Library was also instituted, with the idea of publishing an affordable library of the most important classical works, biographies, religious and philosophical treatments, plays, poems, travel, and adventure. This series eclipsed all competition at the time, and the introduction of paperback books in the 1950s helped to open that market and marked a high point in the industry.

HarperCollins is and has always been a champion of the classics, and the current Collins Classics series follows in this tradition – publishing classical literature that is affordable and available to all. Beautifully packaged, highly collectible, and intended to be reread and enjoyed at every opportunity.

Life & Times

Cinderella and Other Stories

The fairy tales we all grew up with are so familiar to us that it is hard to imagine someone, somewhere, having sat down and actually written them. Perhaps thanks to their modern-day Hollywood adaptations, we barely think of them as books at all. But although tales similar to *Cinderella*, *Sleeping Beauty* and *Puss in Boots* have existed in European oral storytelling traditions for centuries, it took one man, very late in his life, to update them for the modern age and record them for posterity. That man was Charles Perrault.

An Auspicious Start

There is relatively little to be said about Charles Perrault's early years, perhaps because he had a considerably more fortunate childhood than most famous writers. Perrault was born in Paris in 1628, the fifth son of wealthy parents. He was sent to a prestigious school and did well there, becoming, in his own words, 'one of the best students in my class'. 'I took so much pleasure in class debates,' he later recalled in his memoirs, 'that I enjoyed the days we went to school as much as the holidays.' Around the age of fifteen, he left school to study independently for a few years — among other subjects, poetry — during which he also found the time to put together a burlesque translation of a portion of Virgil's *Aeneid*.

But writing was not the career he — or, more to the point, his father — had in mind. Aged twenty-three, and after a fleeting attendance at the University of Orléans ('They were not . . . strict . . . in granting degrees'), Perrault became a lawyer. It was a short-lived endeavour and he never settled into it, abandoning the profession in 1654 to become a government clerk under his brother Pierre. Finding his new job 'not very demanding', Perrault took to visiting libraries and reading poetry, and was inspired to write a poem, 'Le Portrait d'Iris', which was published to positive reviews in 1659.

Although he continued to write and publish poetry, he spent the late 1650s and early 1660s restoring and redesigning a large family estate, as a result of which he came to the attention of Jean-Baptiste Colbert, Louis XIV's superintendent of buildings. Under Colbert's patronage, Perrault rose to a position of significant influence in the royal court, even able to appoint his own brother Claude to design the east wing of the Louvre. He took to commemorating notable royal events in verse.

The Quarrel of the Ancients and the Moderns

By 1671, Perrault was esteemed enough in Parisian society to be elected to the prestigious Académie française, an elite authority established to maintain correct usage of the French language. In this role, he became deeply involved in an academic debate that began as a difference of artistic opinion and quickly developed into a fierce, decades-long war of words between France's most eminent thinkers.

The subject of the debate sounds almost trivial now, but in the late seventeenth century it challenged the very foundations of the Académie française. It centred on a long-held view among academics that no contemporary writer could ever match the talent and excellence of his Classical Greek and Roman predecessors. Perrault was one of a few members who thought differently, and in 1674, after his less enlightened colleagues mounted a denunciation of opera — then a relatively new form of music — he published *Critique de l'Opéra*, a spirited defence that made unfavourable comparisons with ancient works.

The Académie quickly split into two factions, the *Anciens* (among them Nicolas Boileau, Jean Racine and Jean de la Fontaine) and the *Modernes* (led by Perrault), who took to publishing and counter-publishing tracts against the other's thinking. Perrault's *Le Siècle de Louis le Grand* (*The Century of Louis the Great*), published in 1687, was one of the key cases for the prosecution, establishing the *Modernes*' arguably immodest viewpoint that they were living and writing in times of artistic excellence.

The debate continued into the early years of the eighteenth century but Perrault and his supporters ultimately won the day, setting the scene for France to lead the world in literary and artistic experimentation.

Fabulous Beasts

Perrault was briefly married in the 1670s, to Marie Guichon, a woman many decades his junior, and they had four children before she succumbed to an early death. During this period he was influential in advising Louis XIV on his plans for expansion at the Palace of Versailles; perhaps it was becoming a family man that compelled him to talk the king into adding thirty-nine elaborate fountains along the pathways of the Versailles labyrinth, each of them depicting one of Aesop's fables. In a playful twist, the figures were designed to 'converse' with one another by shooting out alternating jets of water. It was an early indication of Perrault's love of old folk tales and memorable characters, although he would not write his first collection until his own children were adults.

This last change in Perrault's meandering career is once

again attributable to the intervention of Jean-Baptiste Colbert, albeit in an indirect way. By the early 1680s Perrault seems to have fallen out of favour with his former patron, and he was gradually pushed aside to make way for Colbert's son. Jobless, widowed, and with his children growing up fast, Perrault turned to writing. He was sixty-nine years old in 1697 when he published *Histoires ou contes du temps passé* or *Les Contes de ma mère l'oye* (*Stories or Tales from Past Times* or *Tales of Mother Goose*).

The tales were modernised, some of them significantly, from both well-known and more obscure European peasant tales as well as from ancient sources — a poke in the eye, it has been argued, to Perrault's *Ancien* colleagues at the Académie française. *The Ridiculous Wishes* and *Donkey-Skin* were stories Perrault had been toying with for a number of years, although both are likely to have been based on folk tales and fables. A handful of the stories had previously appeared in print, notably the *Cinderella* and *Sleeping Beauty* of Giambattista Basile, published in Italy in the 1630s, but the additions and edits made by Perrault were substantial: he gave Cinderella her Fairy Godmother and glass slippers and spared Sleeping Beauty a sexual assault by the king she goes on to marry. He cut the ending in which Puss in Boots fakes his own death to see if he'll get a golden coffin, and gave Little Red Riding Hood her red hood.

Curiously, Perrault published his collection under the name of his teenage son, Pierre Perrault Darmancour. Perhaps, aged almost seventy, and just six years before his death, Perrault was handing over the baton of literary modernism to the next generation.

Charles Perrault died in Paris in 1703. He could little have predicted the legacy of his late literary outpouring, or that many of his adaptations of fables and folk tales would become the definitive texts. Over a century later, when the Brothers Grimm mined European storytelling traditions for their own influential collection, Perrault's *contes* were among the richest sources. If they made changes to his stories to better fit with their own time, one can only assume Perrault would have approved.

CONTENTS

CINDERELLA AND OTHER STORIES

THE SLEEPING BEAUTY
IN THE WOOD

Once upon a time there lived a king and queen who were grieved, more grieved than words can tell, because they had no children. They tried the waters of every country, made vows and pilgrimages, and did everything that could be done, but without result. At last, however, the queen found that her wishes were fulfilled, and in due course she gave birth to a daughter.

A grand christening was held, and all the fairies that could be found in the realm (they numbered seven in all) were invited to be godmothers to the little princess. This was done so that by means of the gifts which each in turn would bestow upon her (in accordance with the fairy custom of those days) the princess might be endowed with every imaginable perfection.

When the christening ceremony was over, all the company returned to the king's palace, where a great banquet was held in honour of the fairies. Places were laid for them in magnificent style, and before each was placed a solid gold casket containing a spoon, fork, and knife of fine gold, set with diamonds and rubies. But just as all were sitting down to table an aged fairy was seen to enter, whom no one had thought to invite—the reason being that for more than fifty years she had never quitted the tower in which she lived, and people had supposed her to be dead or bewitched.

By the king's orders a place was laid for her, but it was impossible to give her a golden casket like the others, for only seven had been made for the seven fairies. The old creature believed that she was intentionally slighted, and muttered threats between her teeth.

She was overheard by one of the young fairies, who was seated near by. The latter, guessing that some mischievous gift might be bestowed upon the little princess, hid behind the tapestry as soon as the company left the table. Her intention was to be the last to speak, and so to have the power of counteracting, as far as possible, any evil which the old fairy might do.

Presently the fairies began to bestow their gifts upon the princess. The youngest ordained that she should be the most beautiful person in the world; the next, that she should have the temper of an angel; the third, that she should do everything with wonderful grace; the fourth, that she should dance to perfection; the fifth, that she should sing like a nightingale; and the sixth, that she should play every kind of music with the utmost skill.

It was now the turn of the aged fairy. Shaking her head, in token of spite rather than of infirmity, she declared that the princess should prick her hand with a spindle, and die of it. A shudder ran through the company at this terrible gift. All eyes were filled with tears.

But at this moment the young fairy stepped forth from behind the tapestry.

'Take comfort, your Majesties,' she cried in a loud voice; 'your daughter shall not die. My power, it is true, is not enough to undo all that my aged kinswoman has decreed: the princess will indeed prick her hand with a spindle. But instead of dying she shall merely fall into a profound slumber that will last a hundred years. At the end of that time a king's son shall come to awaken her.'

The king, in an attempt to avert the unhappy doom pronounced by the old fairy, at once published an edict forbidding all persons, under pain of death, to use a spinning-wheel or keep a spindle in the house.

At the end of fifteen or sixteen years the king and queen happened one day to be away, on pleasure bent. The princess was running about the castle, and going upstairs from room to room she came at length to a garret at the top of a tower, where an old serving-woman sat alone with her distaff, spinning. This good woman had never heard speak of the king's proclamation forbidding the use of spinning-wheels.

'What are you doing, my good woman?' asked the princess.

'I am spinning, my pretty child,' replied the dame, not knowing who she was.

'Oh, what fun!' rejoined the princess; 'how do you do it? Let me try and see if I can do it equally well.'

Partly because she was too hasty, partly because she was a little heedless, but also because the fairy decree had ordained it, no sooner had she seized the spindle than she pricked her hand and fell down in a swoon.

In great alarm the good dame cried out for help. People came running from every quarter to the princess. They threw water on her face, chafed her with their hands, and rubbed her temples with the royal essence of Hungary. But nothing would restore her.

Then the king, who had been brought upstairs by the commotion, remembered the fairy prophecy. Feeling certain that what had happened was inevitable, since the fairies had decreed it, he gave orders that the princess should be placed in the finest apartment in the palace, upon a bed embroidered in gold and silver.

You would have thought her an angel, so fair was she to behold. The trance had not taken away the lovely colour of her complexion. Her cheeks were delicately flushed, her lips like coral. Her eyes, indeed, were closed, but her gentle breathing could be heard, and it was therefore plain that she was not dead. The king commanded that she should be left to sleep in peace until the hour of her awakening should come.

When the accident happened to the princess, the good fairy who had saved her life by condemning her to sleep a hundred years was in the kingdom of Mataquin, twelve thousand leagues away. She was instantly warned of it, however, by a little dwarf who had a pair of seven-league boots, which are boots that enable one to cover seven leagues at a single step. The fairy set off at once, and within an hour her chariot of fire, drawn by dragons, was seen approaching.

The king handed her down from her chariot, and she approved of all that he had done. But being gifted with great powers of foresight, she bethought herself that when the princess came to be awakened, she would be much distressed to find herself all alone in the old castle. And this is what she did.

She touched with her wand everybody (except the king and queen) who was in the castle—governesses, maids of honour, ladies-in-waiting, gentlemen, officers, stewards, cooks, scullions, errand boys, guards, porters, pages, footmen. She touched likewise all the horses in the stables, with their grooms, the big mastiffs in the courtyard, and little Puff, the pet dog of the princess, who was lying on the bed beside his mistress. The moment she had touched them they all fell asleep, to awaken only at the same moment as their mistress. Thus they would always be ready with their service whenever she should require it. The very spits before the fire, loaded with partridges and pheasants, subsided into slumber, and the fire as well. All was done in a moment, for the fairies do not take long over their work.

Then the king and queen kissed their dear child, without waking her, and left the castle. Proclamations were issued, forbidding any approach to it, but these warnings were not needed, for within a quarter of an hour there grew up all round the park so vast a quantity of trees big and small, with interlacing brambles and thorns, that neither man nor beast could penetrate them. The tops alone of the castle towers could be seen, and these only from a distance. Thus did the fairy's magic contrive that the princess, during all the time of her slumber, should have nought whatever to fear from prying eyes.

At the end of a hundred years the throne had passed to another family from that of the sleeping princess. One day the king's son chanced to go a-hunting that way, and seeing in the distance some towers in the midst of a large and dense forest, he asked what they were. His attendants told him in reply the various stories which they had heard. Some said there was an old castle haunted by ghosts, others that all the witches of the neighbourhood held their revels there. The favourite tale was that in the castle lived an ogre, who carried thither all the children whom he could catch. There he devoured them at his leisure, and since he was the only person who could force a passage through the wood nobody had been able to pursue him.

While the prince was wondering what to believe, an old peasant took up the tale.

'Your Highness.' said he, 'more than fifty years ago I heard my father say that in this castle lies a princess, the most beautiful that has ever been seen. It is her doom to sleep there for a hundred years, and then to be awakened by a king's son, for whose coming she waits.'

This story fired the young prince. He jumped immediately to the conclusion that it was for him to see so gay an adventure through, and impelled alike by the wish for love and glory, he resolved to set about it on the spot.

Hardly had he taken a step towards the wood when the tall trees, the brambles and the thorns, separated of themselves and made a path for him. He turned in the direction of the castle, and espied it at the end of a long avenue. This avenue he entered, and was surprised to notice that the trees closed up again as soon as he had passed, so that none of his retinue were able to follow him. A young and gallant prince is always brave, however; so he continued on his way, and presently reached a large fore-court.

The sight that now met his gaze was enough to fill him with an icy fear. The silence of the place was dreadful, and death seemed all about him. The recumbent figures of men and animals had all the appearance of being lifeless, until he perceived by the pimply noses and ruddy faces of the porters that they merely slept. It was plain, too, from their glasses, in which were still some dregs of wine, that they had fallen asleep while drinking.

The prince made his way into a great courtyard, paved with marble, and mounting the staircase entered the guard-room. Here the guards were lined up on either side in two ranks, their muskets on their shoulders, snoring their hardest. Through several apartments crowded with ladies and gentlemen in waiting, some seated, some standing, but all asleep, he pushed on, and so came at last to a chamber which was decked all over with gold. There he encountered the most beautiful sight he had ever seen. Reclining upon a bed, the curtains of which on every side were drawn back, was a princess of seemingly some fifteen or sixteen summers, whose radiant beauty had an almost unearthly lustre.

Trembling in his admiration he drew near and went on his knees beside her. At the same moment, the hour of disenchantment having come, the princess awoke, and bestowed upon him a look more tender than a first glance might seem to warrant.

'Is it you, dear prince?' she said; 'you have been long in coming!'

Charmed by these words, and especially by the manner in which they were said, the prince scarcely knew how to express his delight and gratification. He declared that he loved her better than he loved himself. His words were faltering, but they pleased the more for that. The less there is of eloquence, the more there is of love.

Her embarrassment was less than his, and that is not to be wondered at, since she had had time to think of what she would say to him. It seems (although the story says nothing about it) that the good fairy had beguiled her long slumber with pleasant dreams. To be brief, after four hours of talking they had not succeeded in uttering one half of the things they had to say to each other.

Now the whole palace had awakened with the princess. Every one went about his business, and since they were not all in love they presently began to feel mortally hungry. The lady-in-waiting, who was suffering like the rest, at length lost patience, and in a loud voice called out to the princess that supper was served.

The princess was already fully dressed, and in most magnificent style. As he helped her to rise, the prince refrained from telling her that her clothes, with the straight collar which she wore, were like those to which his grandmother had been accustomed. And in truth, they in no way detracted from her beauty.

They passed into an apartment hung with mirrors, and were there served with supper by the stewards of the household, while the fiddles and oboes played some old music—and played it remarkably well, considering they had not played at all for just upon a hundred years. A little later, when supper was over, the chaplain married them in the castle chapel, and in due course, attended by the courtiers in waiting, they retired to rest.

They slept but little, however. The princess, indeed, had not much need of sleep, and as soon as morning came the prince took his leave of her. He returned to the city, and told his father, who was awaiting him with some anxiety, that he had lost himself while hunting in the forest, but had obtained some black bread and cheese from a charcoal-burner, in whose hovel he had passed the night. His royal father, being of an easy-going nature, believed the tale, but his mother was not so easily hoodwinked. She noticed that he now went hunting every day, and that he always had an excuse handy when he had slept two or three nights from home. She felt certain, therefore, that he had some love affair.

Two whole years passed since the marriage of the prince and princess, and during that time they had two children. The first, a daughter, was called 'Dawn' while the second, a boy, was named 'Day' because he seemed even more beautiful than his sister.

Many a time the queen told her son that he ought to settle down in life. She tried in this way to make him confide in her, but he did not dare to trust her with his secret. Despite the affection which he bore her, he was afraid of his mother, for she came of a race of ogres, and the king had only married her for her wealth.

It was whispered at the Court that she had ogrish instincts, and that when little children were near her she had the greatest difficulty in the world to keep herself from pouncing on them.

No wonder the prince was reluctant to say a word.

But at the end of two years the king died, and the prince found himself on the throne. He then made public announcement of his marriage, and went in state to fetch his royal consort from her castle. With her two children beside her she made a triumphal entry into the capital of her husband's realm.

Some time afterwards the king declared war on his neighbour, the Emperor Cantalabutte. He appointed the queen-mother as regent in his absence, and entrusted his wife and children to her care.

He expected to be away at the war for the whole of the summer, and as soon as he was gone the queen-mother sent her daughter-in-law and the two children to a country mansion in the forest. This she did that she might be able the more easily to gratify her horrible longings. A few days later she went there herself, and in the evening summoned the chief steward.

'For my dinner to-morrow,' she told him, 'I will eat little Dawn.'

'Oh, Madam!' exclaimed the steward.

'That is my will,' said the queen; and she spoke in the tones of an ogre who longs for raw meat.

'You will serve her with piquant sauce,' she added.

The poor man, seeing plainly that it was useless to trifle with an ogress, took his big knife and went up to little Dawn's chamber. She was at that time four years old, and when she came running with a smile to greet him, flinging her arms round his neck and coaxing him to give her some sweets, he burst into tears, and let the knife fall from his hand.

Presently he went down to the yard behind the house, and slaughtered a young lamb. For this he made so delicious a sauce that his mistress declared she had never eaten anything so good.

At the same time the steward carried little Dawn to his wife, and bade the latter hide her in the quarters which they had below the yard.

Eight days later the wicked queen summoned her steward again.

'For my supper,' she announced, 'I will eat little Day.'

The steward made no answer, being determined to trick her as he had done previously. He went in search of little Day, whom he found with a tiny foil in his hand, making brave passes—though he was but three years old—at a big monkey. He carried him off to his wife, who stowed him away in hiding with little Dawn. To the ogress the steward served up, in place of Day, a young kid so tender that she found it surpassingly delicious.

So far, so good. But there came an evening when this evil queen again addressed the steward.

'I have a mind,' she said, 'to eat the queen with the same sauce as you served with her children.'

This time the poor steward despaired of being able to practise another deception. The young queen was twenty years old, without counting the hundred years she had been asleep. Her skin, though white and beautiful, had become a little tough, and what animal could he possibly find that would correspond to her? He made up his mind that if he would save his own life he must kill the queen, and went upstairs to her apartment determined to do the deed once and for all. Goading himself into a rage he drew his knife and entered the young queen's chamber, but a reluctance to give her no moment of grace made him repeat respectfully the command which he had received from the queen-mother.

'Do it! do it!' she cried, baring her neck to him; 'carry out the order you have been given! Then once more I shall see my children, my poor children that I loved so much!'

Nothing had been said to her when the children were stolen away, and she believed them to be dead.

The poor steward was overcome by compassion. 'No, no, Madam.' he declared; 'you shall not die, but you shall certainly see your children again. That will be in my quarters, where I have hidden them. I shall make the queen eat a young hind in place of you, and thus trick her once more.'

Without more ado he led her to his quarters, and leaving her there to embrace and weep over her children, proceeded to cook a hind with such art that the queen-mother ate it for her supper with as much appetite as if it had indeed been the young queen.

The queen-mother felt well satisfied with her cruel deeds, and planned to tell the king, on his return, that savage wolves had devoured his consort and his children. It was her habit, however, to prowl often about the courts and alleys of the mansion, in the hope of scenting raw meat, and one evening she heard the little boy Day crying in a basement cellar. The child was weeping because his mother had threatened to whip him for some naughtiness, and she heard at the same time the voice of Dawn begging forgiveness for her brother.

The ogress recognised the voices of the queen and her children, and was enraged to find she had been tricked. The next morning, in tones so affrighting that all trembled, she ordered a huge vat to be brought into the middle of the courtyard. This she filled with vipers and toads, with snakes and serpents of every kind, intending to cast into it the queen and her children, and the steward with his wife and serving-girl. By her command these were brought forward, with their hands tied behind their backs.

There they were, and her minions were making ready to cast them into the vat, when into the courtyard rode the king! Nobody had expected him so soon, but he had travelled post-haste. Filled with amazement, he demanded to know what this horrible spectacle meant. None dared tell him, and at that moment the ogress, enraged at what confronted her, threw herself head foremost into the vat, and was devoured on the instant by the hideous creatures she had placed in it.

The king could not but be sorry, for after all she was his mother; but it was not long before he found ample consolation in his beautiful wife and children.

PUSS IN BOOTS

A certain miller had three sons, and when he died the sole worldly goods which he bequeathed to them were his mill, his ass, and his cat. This little legacy was very quickly divided up, and you may be quite sure that neither notary nor attorney were called in to help, for they would speedily have grabbed it all for themselves.

The eldest son took the mill, and the second son took the ass. Consequently all that remained for the youngest son was the cat, and he was not a little disappointed at receiving such a miserable portion.

'My brothers,' said he, 'will be able to get a decent living by joining forces, but for my part, as soon as I have eaten my cat and made a muff out of his skin, I am bound to die of hunger.'

These remarks were overheard by Puss, who pretended not to have been listening, and said very soberly and seriously:

'There is not the least need for you to worry, Master. All you have to do is to give me a pouch, and get a pair of boots made for me so that I can walk in the woods. You will find then that your share is not so bad after all.'

Now this cat had often shown himself capable of performing cunning tricks. When catching rats and mice, for example, he would hide himself amongst the meal and hang downwards by the feet as though he were dead. His master, therefore, though he did not build too much on what the cat had said, felt some hope of being assisted in his miserable plight.

On receiving the boots which he had asked for, Puss gaily pulled them on. Then he hung the pouch round his neck, and holding the cords which tied it in front of him with his paws, he sallied forth to a warren where rabbits abounded. Placing some bran and lettuce in the pouch, he stretched himself out and lay as if dead. His plan was to wait until some young rabbit, unlearned in worldly wisdom, should come and rummage in the pouch for the eatables which he had placed there.

Hardly had he laid himself down when things fell out as he wished. A stupid young rabbit went into the pouch, and Master Puss, pulling the cords tight, killed him on the instant.

Well satisfied with his capture, Puss departed to the king's palace. There he demanded an audience, and was ushered upstairs. He entered the royal apartment, and bowed profoundly to the king.

'I bring you, Sire.' said he, 'a rabbit from the warren of the marquis of Carabas (such was the title he invented for his master), which I am bidden to present to you on his behalf.'

'Tell your master,' replied the king, 'that I thank him, and am pleased by his attention.'

Another time the cat hid himself in a wheatfield, keeping the mouth of his bag wide open. Two partridges ventured in, and by pulling the cords tight he captured both of them. Off he went and presented them to the king, just as he had done with the rabbit from the warren. His Majesty was not less gratified by the brace of partridges, and handed the cat a present for himself.

For two or three months Puss went on in this way, every

now and again taking to the king, as a present from his master, some game which he had caught. There came a day when he learned that the king intended to take his daughter, who was the most beautiful princess in the world, for an excursion along the river bank.

'If you will do as I tell you,' said Puss to his master, 'your fortune is made. You have only to go and bathe in the river at the spot which I shall point out to you. Leave the rest to me.'

The marquis of Carabas had no idea what plan was afoot, but did as the cat had directed.

While he was bathing the king drew near, and Puss at once began to cry out at the top of his voice:

'Help! help! the marquis of Carabas is drowning!'

At these shouts the king put his head out of the carriage window. He recognised the cat who had so often brought him game, and bade his escort go speedily to the help of the marquis of Carabas.

While they were pulling the poor marquis out of the river, Puss approached the carriage and explained to the king that while his master was bathing robbers had come and taken away his clothes, though he had cried 'Stop, thief!' at the top of his voice. As a matter of fact, the rascal had hidden them under a big stone. The king at once commanded the keepers of his wardrobe to go and select a suit of his finest clothes for the marquis of Carabas.

The king received the marquis with many compliments, and as the fine clothes which the latter had just put on set off his good looks (for he was handsome and comely in appearance), the king's daughter found him very much to her liking. Indeed, the marquis of Carabas had not bestowed more than two or three respectful but sentimental glances upon her when she fell madly in love with him. The king invited him to enter the coach and join the party.

Delighted to see his plan so successfully launched, the

cat went on ahead, and presently came upon some peasants who were mowing a field.

'Listen, my good fellows,' said he; 'if you do not tell the king that the field which you are mowing belongs to the marquis of Carabas, you will all be chopped up into little pieces like mince-meat.'

In due course the king asked the mowers to whom the field on which they were at work belonged.

'It is the property of the marquis of Carabas,' they all cried with one voice, for the threat from Puss had frightened them.

'You have inherited a fine estate,' the king remarked to Carabas.

'As you see for yourself, Sire,' replied the marquis; 'this is a meadow which never fails to yield an abundant crop each year.'

Still travelling ahead, the cat came upon some harvesters.

'Listen, my good fellows,' said he; 'if you do not declare that every one of these fields belongs to the marquis of Carabas, you will all be chopped up into little bits like mince-meat.'

The king came by a moment later, and wished to know who was the owner of the fields in sight.

'It is the marquis of Carabas,' cried the harvesters.

At this the king was more pleased than ever with the marquis.

Preceding the coach on its journey, the cat made the same threat to all whom he met, and the king grew astonished at the great wealth of the marquis of Carabas.

Finally Master Puss reached a splendid castle, which belonged to an ogre. He was the richest ogre that had ever been known, for all the lands through which the king had passed were part of the castle domain.

The cat had taken care to find out who this ogre was, and what powers he possessed. He now asked for an interview, declaring that he was unwilling to pass so close to the castle without having the honour of paying his respects to the owner.

The ogre received him as civilly as an ogre can, and bade him sit down.

'I have been told,' said Puss, 'that you have the power to change yourself into any kind of animal—for example, that you can transform yourself into a lion or an elephant.'

'That is perfectly true,' said the ogre, curtly; 'and just to prove it you shall see me turn into a lion.'

Puss was so frightened on seeing a lion before him that he sprang on to the roof—not without difficulty and danger, for his boots were not meant for walking on the tiles.

Perceiving presently that the ogre had abandoned his transformation, Puss descended, and owned to having been thoroughly frightened.

'I have also been told,' he added, 'but I can scarcely believe it, that you have the further power to take the shape of the smallest animals—for example, that you can change yourself into a rat or a mouse. I confess that to me it seems quite impossible.'

'Impossible?' cried the ogre; 'you shall see!' And in the same moment he changed himself into a mouse, which began to run about the floor. No sooner did Puss see it than he pounced on it and ate it.

Presently the king came along, and noticing the ogre's beautiful mansion desired to visit it. The cat heard the rumble of the coach as it crossed the castle drawbridge, and running out to the courtyard cried to the king:

'Welcome, your Majesty, to the castle of the marquis of Carabas!'

'What's that?' cried the king. 'Is this castle also yours, marquis? Nothing could be finer than this courtyard and the buildings which I see all about. With your permission we will go inside and look round.'

The marquis gave his hand to the young princess, and

followed the king as he led the way up the staircase. Entering a great hall they found there a magnificent collation. This had been prepared by the ogre for some friends who were to pay him a visit that very day. The latter had not dared to enter when they learned that the king was there.

The king was now quite as charmed with the excellent qualities of the marquis of Carabas as his daughter. The latter was completely captivated by him. Noting the great wealth of which the marquis was evidently possessed, and having quaffed several cups of wine, he turned to his host, saying:

'It rests with you, marquis, whether you will be my son-in-law.'

The marquis, bowing very low, accepted the honour which the king bestowed upon him. The very same day he married the princess.

Puss became a personage of great importance, and gave up hunting mice, except for amusement.

LITTLE TOM THUMB

Once upon a time there lived a wood-cutter and his wife, who had seven children, all boys. The eldest was only ten years old, and the youngest was seven. People were astonished that the wood-cutter had had so many children in so short a time, but the reason was that his wife delighted in children, and never had less than two at a time.

They were very poor, and their seven children were a great tax on them, for none of them was yet able to earn his own living. And they were troubled also because the youngest was very delicate and could not speak a word. They mistook for stupidity what was in reality a mark of good sense.

This youngest boy was very little. At his birth he was scarcely bigger than a man's thumb, and he was called in consequence 'Little Tom Thumb.' The poor child was the scapegoat of the family, and got the blame for everything. All the same, he was the sharpest and shrewdest of the brothers, and if he spoke but little he listened much.

There came a very bad year, when the famine was so great that these poor people resolved to get rid of their family. One evening, after the children had gone to bed, the wood-cutter was sitting in the chimney-corner with his wife. His heart was heavy with sorrow as he said to her:

'It must be plain enough to you that we can no longer feed our children. I cannot see them die of hunger before my eyes, and I have made up my mind to take them to-morrow to the forest and lose them there. It will be easy enough to manage, for while they are amusing themselves by collecting faggots we have only to disappear without their seeing us.'

'Ah!' cried the wood-cutter's wife, 'do you mean to say you are capable of letting your own children be lost?'

In vain did her husband remind her of their terrible poverty; she could not agree. She was poor, but she was their mother. In the end, however, reflecting what a grief it would be to see them die of hunger, she consented to the plan, and went weeping to bed.

Little Tom Thumb had heard all that was said. Having discovered, when in bed, that serious talk was going on, he had got up softly, and had slipped under his father's stool in order to listen without being seen. He went back to bed, but did not sleep a wink for the rest of the night, thinking over what he had better do. In the morning he rose very early and went to the edge of a brook. There he filled his pockets with little white pebbles and came quickly home again.

They all set out, and little Tom Thumb said not a word to his brothers of what he knew.

They went into a forest which was so dense that when only ten paces apart they could not see each other. The wood-cutter set about his work, and the children began to collect twigs to make faggots. Presently the father and mother, seeing them busy at their task, edged gradually away, and then hurried off in haste along a little narrow footpath.

When the children found they were alone they began to

cry and call out with all their might. Little Tom Thumb let them cry, being confident that they would get back home again. For on the way he had dropped the little white stones which he carried in his pocket all along the path.

'Don't be afraid, brothers,' he said presently; 'our parents have left us here, but I will take you home again. Just follow me.'

They fell in behind him, and he led them straight to their house by the same path which they had taken to the forest. At first they dared not go in, but placed themselves against the door, where they could hear everything their father and mother were saying.

Now the wood-cutter and his wife had no sooner reached home than the lord of the manor sent them a sum of ten crowns which had been owing from him for a long time, and of which they had given up hope. This put new life into them, for the poor creatures were dying of hunger.

The wood-cutter sent his wife off to the butcher at once, and as it was such a long time since they had had anything to eat, she bought three times as much meat as a supper for two required.

When they found themselves once more at table, the wood-cutter's wife began to lament.

'Alas! where are our poor children now?' she said; 'they could make a good meal off what we have over. Mind you, William, it was you who wished to lose them: I declared over and over again that we should repent it. What are they doing now in that forest? Merciful heavens, perhaps the wolves have already eaten them! A monster you must be to lose your children in this way!'

At last the wood-cutter lost patience, for she repeated more than twenty times that he would repent it, and that she had told him so. He threatened to beat her if she did not hold her tongue.

It was not that the wood-cutter was less grieved than

his wife, but she browbeat him, and he was of the same opinion as many other people, who like a woman to have the knack of saying the right thing, but not the trick of being always in the right.

'Alas!' cried the wood-cutter's wife, bursting into tears, 'where are now my children, my poor children?'

She said it once so loud that the children at the door heard it plainly. Together they all called out:

'Here we are! Here we are!'

She rushed to open the door for them, and exclaimed, as she embraced them:

'How glad I am to see you again, dear children! You must be very tired and very hungry. And you, Peterkin, how muddy you are—come and let me wash you!'

This Peterkin was her eldest son. She loved him more than all the others because he was inclined to be red-headed, and she herself was rather red.

They sat down at the table and ate with an appetite which it did their parents good to see. They all talked at once, as they recounted the fears they had felt in the forest.

The good souls were delighted to have their children with them again, and the pleasure continued as long as the ten crowns lasted. But when the money was all spent they relapsed into their former sadness. They again resolved to lose the children, and to lead them much further away than they had done the first time, so as to do the job thoroughly. But though they were careful not to speak openly about it, their conversation did not escape little Tom Thumb, who made up his mind to get out of the situation as he had done on the former occasion.

But though he got up early to go and collect his little stones, he found the door of the house doubly locked, and he could not carry out his plan.

He could not think what to do until the wood-cutter's wife gave them each a piece of bread for breakfast. Then it occurred to him to use the bread in place of the stones, by throwing crumbs along the path which they took, and he tucked it tight in his pocket.

Their parents led them into the thickest and darkest part of the forest, and as soon as they were there slipped away by a side-path and left them. This did not much trouble little Tom Thumb, for he believed he could easily find the way back by means of the bread which he had scattered wherever he walked. But to his dismay he could not discover a single crumb. The birds had come along and eaten it all.

They were in sore trouble now, for with every step they strayed further, and became more and more entangled in the forest. Night came on and a terrific wind arose, which filled them with dreadful alarm. On every side they seemed to hear nothing but the howling of wolves which were coming to eat them up. They dared not speak or move.

In addition it began to rain so heavily that they were soaked to the skin. At every step they tripped and fell on the wet ground, getting up again covered with mud, not knowing what to do with their hands.

Little Tom Thumb climbed to the top of a tree, in an endeavour to see something. Looking all about him he espied, far away on the other side of the forest, a little light like that of a candle. He got down from the tree, and was terribly disappointed to find that when he was on the ground he could see nothing at all.

After they had walked some distance in the direction of the light, however, he caught a glimpse of it again as they were nearing the edge of the forest. At last they reached the house where the light was burning, but not without much anxiety, for every time they had to go down into a hollow they lost sight of it.

They knocked at the door, and a good dame opened to them. She asked them what they wanted.

Little Tom Thumb explained that they were poor children who had lost their way in the forest, and begged her, for pity's sake, to give them a night's lodging.

Noticing what bonny children they all were, the woman began to cry.

'Alas, my poor little dears!' she said; 'you do not know the place you have come to! Have you not heard that this is the house of an ogre who eats little children?'

'Alas, madam!' answered little Tom Thumb, trembling like all the rest of his brothers, 'what shall we do? One thing is very certain: if you do not take us in, the wolves of the forest will devour us this very night, and that being so we should prefer to be eaten by your husband. Perhaps he may take pity on us, if you will plead for us.'

The ogre's wife, thinking she might be able to hide them from her husband till the next morning, allowed them to come in, and put them to warm near a huge fire, where a whole sheep was cooking on the spit for the ogre's supper.

Just as they were beginning to get warm they heard two or three great bangs at the door. The ogre had returned. His wife hid them quickly under the bed and ran to open the door.

The first thing the ogre did was to ask whether supper was ready and the wine opened. Then without ado he sat down to table. Blood was still dripping from the sheep, but it seemed all the better to him for that. He sniffed to right and left, declaring that he could smell fresh flesh.

'Indeed!' said his wife. 'It must be the calf which I have just dressed that you smell.'

'*I smell fresh flesh*, I tell you!' shouted the ogre, eyeing his wife askance; 'and there is something going on here which I do not understand.'

With these words he got up from the table and went straight to the bed.

'Aha!' said he; 'so this is the way you deceive me, wicked

woman that you are! I have a very great mind to eat you too! It's lucky for you that you are old and tough! I am expecting three ogre friends of mine to pay me a visit in the next few days, and here is a tasty dish which will just come in nicely for them!'

One after another he dragged the children out from under the bed.

The poor things threw themselves on their knees, imploring mercy; but they had to deal with the most cruel of all ogres. Far from pitying them, he was already devouring them with his eyes, and repeating to his wife that when cooked with a good sauce they would make most dainty morsels.

Off he went to get a large knife, which he sharpened, as he drew near the poor children, on a long stone in his left hand.

He had already seized one of them when his wife called out to him. 'What do you want to do it now for?' she said; 'will it not be time enough to-morrow?'

'Hold your tongue,' replied the ogre; 'they will be all the more tender.'

'But you have such a lot of meat,' rejoined his wife; 'look, there are a calf, two sheep, and half a pig.'

'You are right,' said the ogre; 'give them a good supper to fatten them up, and take them to bed.'

The good woman was overjoyed and brought them a splendid supper; but the poor little wretches were so cowed with fright that they could not eat.

As for the ogre, he went back to his drinking, very pleased to have such good entertainment for his friends. He drank a dozen cups more than usual, and was obliged to go off to bed early, for the wine had gone somewhat to his head.

Now the ogre had seven daughters who as yet were only children. These little ogresses all had the most lovely complexions, for, like their father, they ate fresh meat. But they had little round grey eyes, crooked noses, and very large mouths, with long and exceedingly sharp teeth, set far apart. They were not so very wicked at present, but they showed great promise, for already they were in the habit of killing little children to suck their blood.

They had gone to bed early, and were all seven in a great bed, each with a crown of gold upon her head.

In the same room there was another bed, equally large. Into this the ogre's wife put the seven little boys, and then went to sleep herself beside her husband.

Little Tom Thumb was fearful lest the ogre should suddenly regret that he had not cut the throats of himself and his brothers the evening before. Having noticed that the ogre's daughters all had golden crowns upon their heads, he got up in the middle of the night and softly placed his own cap and those of his brothers on their heads. Before doing so, he carefully removed the crowns of gold, putting them on his own and his brothers' heads. In this way, if the ogre were to feel like slaughtering them that night he would mistake the girls for the boys, and *vice versa*.

Things fell out just as he had anticipated. The ogre, waking up at midnight, regretted that he had postponed till the morrow what he could have done overnight. Jumping briskly out of bed, he seized his knife, crying: 'Now then, let's see how the little rascals are; we won't make the same mistake twice!'

He groped his way up to his daughters' room, and approached the bed in which were the seven little boys. All were sleeping, with the exception of little Tom Thumb, who was numb with fear when he felt the ogre's hand, as it touched the head of each brother in turn, reach his own.

'Upon my word.' said the ogre, as he felt the golden crowns; 'a nice job I was going to make of it! It is very evident that I drank a little too much last night!'

Forthwith he went to the bed where his daughters were, and here he felt the little boys' caps.

'Aha, here are the little scamps!' he cried; 'now for a smart bit of work!'

With these words, and without a moment's hesitation, he cut the throats of his seven daughters, and well satisfied with his work went back to bed beside his wife.

No sooner did little Tom Thumb hear him snoring than he woke up his brothers, bidding them dress quickly and follow him. They crept quietly down to the garden, and jumped from the wall. All through the night they ran in haste and terror, without the least idea of where they were going.

When the ogre woke up he said to his wife:

'Go upstairs and dress those little rascals who were here last night.'

The ogre's wife was astonished at her husband's kindness, never doubting that he meant her to go and put on their clothes. She went upstairs, and was horrified to discover her seven daughters bathed in blood, with their throats cut.

She fell at once into a swoon, which is the way of most women in similar circumstances.

The ogre, thinking his wife was very long in carrying out his orders, went up to help her, and was no less astounded than his wife at the terrible spectacle which confronted him.

'What's this I have done?' he exclaimed. 'I will be revenged on the wretches, and quickly, too!'

He threw a jugful of water over his wife's face, and having brought her round ordered her to fetch his seven-league boots, so that he might overtake the children.

He set off over the countryside, and strode far and wide until he came to the road along which the poor children were travelling. They were not more than a few yards from their home when they saw the ogre striding from hill-top to hill-top, and stepping over rivers as though they were merely tiny streams.

Little Tom Thumb espied near at hand a cave in some rocks. In this he hid his brothers, and himself followed them in, while continuing to keep a watchful eye upon the movements of the ogre.

Now the ogre was feeling very tired after so much fruitless marching (for seven-league boots are very fatiguing to their wearer), and felt like taking a little rest. As it happened, he went and sat down on the very rock beneath which the little boys were hiding. Overcome with weariness, he had not sat there long before he fell asleep and began to snore so terribly that the poor children were as frightened as when he had held his great knife to their throats.

Little Tom Thumb was not so alarmed. He told his brothers to flee at once to their home while the ogre was still sleeping soundly, and not to worry about him. They took his advice and ran quickly home.

Little Tom Thumb now approached the ogre and gently pulled off his boots, which he at once donned himself. The boots were very heavy and very large, but being enchanted boots they had the faculty of growing larger or smaller according to the leg they had to suit. Consequently they always fitted as though they had been made for the wearer.

He went straight to the ogre's house, where he found the ogre's wife weeping over her murdered daughters.

'Your husband,' said little Tom Thumb, 'is in great danger, for he has been captured by a gang of thieves, and the latter have sworn to kill him if he does not hand over all his gold and silver. Just as they had the dagger at his throat, he caught sight of me and begged me to come to you and thus rescue him from his terrible plight. You are to give me everything of value which he possesses, without keeping back a thing, otherwise he will be slain without mercy. As the matter is urgent he wished me to wear his seven-league boots, to save time, and also to prove to you that I am no impostor.'

The ogre's wife, in great alarm, gave him immediately all that she had, for although this was an ogre who devoured little children, he was by no means a bad husband.

Little Tom Thumb, laden with all the ogre's wealth, forthwith repaired to his father's house, where he was received with great joy.

Many people do not agree about this last adventure, and pretend that little Tom Thumb never committed this theft from the ogre, and only took the seven-league boots, about which he had no compunction, since they were only used by the ogre for catching little children. These folks assert that they are in a position to know, having been guests at the wood-cutter's cottage. They further say that when little Tom Thumb had put on the ogre's boots, he went off to the Court, where he knew there was great anxiety concerning the result of a battle which was being fought by an army two hundred leagues away.

They say that he went to the king and undertook, if desired, to bring news of the army before the day was out; and that the king promised him a large sum of money if he could carry out his project.

Little Tom Thumb brought news that very night, and this first errand having brought him into notice, he made as much money as he wished. For not only did the king pay him handsomely to carry orders to the army, but many ladies at the court gave him anything he asked to get them news of their lovers, and this was his greatest source of income. He was occasionally entrusted by wives with letters to their husbands, but they paid him so badly, and this branch of the business brought him in so little, that he did not even bother to reckon what he made from it.

After acting as courier for some time, and amassing great wealth thereby, little Tom Thumb returned to his father's house, and was there greeted with the greatest joy imaginable. He made all his family comfortable, buying newly-created positions for his father and brothers. In this way he set them all up, not forgetting at the same time to look well after himself.

THE FAIRIES

Once upon a time there lived a widow with two daughters. The elder was often mistaken for her mother, so like her was she both in nature and in looks; parent and child being so disagreeable and arrogant that no one could live with them.

The younger girl, who took after her father in the gentleness and sweetness of her disposition, was also one of the prettiest girls imaginable. The mother doted on the elder daughter—naturally enough, since she resembled her so closely—and disliked the younger one as intensely. She made the latter live in the kitchen and work hard from morning till night.

One of the poor child's many duties was to go twice a day and draw water from a spring a good half-mile away, bringing it back in a large pitcher. One day when she was at the spring an old woman came up and begged for a drink.

'Why, certainly, good mother,' the pretty lass replied. Rinsing her pitcher, she drew some water from the cleanest part of the spring and handed it to the dame, lifting up the jug so that she might drink the more easily.

Now this old woman was a fairy, who had taken the form of a poor village dame to see just how far the girl's good nature would go. 'You are so pretty.' she said, when she had finished drinking, 'and so polite, that I am determined to bestow a gift upon you. This is the boon I grant you: with every word that you utter there shall fall from your mouth either a flower or a precious stone.'

When the girl reached home she was scolded by her mother for being so long in coming back from the spring.

'I am sorry to have been so long, mother,' said the poor child.

As she spoke these words there fell from her mouth three roses, three pearls, and three diamonds.

'What's this?' cried her mother; 'did I see pearls and diamonds dropping out of your mouth? What does this mean, dear daughter?' (This was the first time she had ever addressed her daughter affectionately.)

The poor child told a simple tale of what had happened, and in speaking scattered diamonds right and left.

'Really!' said her mother. 'I must send my own child there. Come here, Fanchon; look what comes out of your sister's mouth whenever she speaks! Wouldn't you like to be able to do the same? All you have to do is to go and draw some water at the spring, and when a poor woman asks you for a drink, give it her very nicely.'

'Oh, indeed!' replied the ill-mannered girl; 'don't you wish you may see me going there!'

'I tell you that you are to go.' said her mother, 'and to go this instant.'

Very sulkily the girl went off, taking with her the best silver flagon in the house. No sooner had she reached the spring than she saw a lady, magnificently attired, who came towards her from the forest, and asked for a drink. This was the same fairy who had appeared to her sister, masquerading now as a princess in order to see how far this girl's ill-nature would carry her.

'Do you think I have come here just to get you a drink?' said the loutish damsel, arrogantly. 'I suppose you think I brought a silver flagon here specially for that purpose—it's so likely, isn't it? Drink from the spring, if you want to!'

'You are not very polite.' said the fairy, displaying no sign of anger. 'Well, in return for your lack of courtesy I decree that for every word you utter a snake or a toad shall drop out of your mouth.'

The moment her mother caught sight of her coming back she cried out, 'Well, daughter?'

'Well, mother?' replied the rude girl. As she spoke a viper and a toad were spat out of her mouth.

'Gracious heavens!' cried her mother; 'What do I see? Her sister is the cause of this, and I will make her pay for it!'

Off she ran to thrash the poor child, but the latter fled away and hid in the forest near by. The king's son met her on his way home from hunting, and noticing how pretty she was inquired what she was doing all alone, and what she was weeping about.

'Alas, sir,' she cried; 'my mother has driven me from home!'

As she spoke the prince saw four or five pearls and as many diamonds fall from her mouth. He begged her to tell him how this came about, and she told him the whole story.

The king's son fell in love with her, and reflecting that such a gift as had been bestowed upon her was worth more than any dowry which another maiden might bring him, he took her to the palace of his royal father, and there married her.

As for the sister, she made herself so hateful that even her mother drove her out of the house. Nowhere could the wretched girl find any one who would take her in, and at last she lay down in the forest and died.

RICKY OF THE TUFT

Once upon a time there was a queen who bore a son so ugly and misshapen that for some time it was doubtful if he would have human form at all. But a fairy who was present at his birth promised that he should have plenty of brains, and added that by virtue of the gift which she had just bestowed upon him he would be able to impart to the person whom he should love best the same degree of intelligence which he possessed himself.

This somewhat consoled the poor queen, who was greatly disappointed at having brought into the world such a hideous brat. And indeed, no sooner did the child begin to speak than his sayings proved to be full of shrewdness, while all that he did was somehow so clever that he charmed every one.

I forgot to mention that when he was born he had a little tuft of hair upon his head. For this reason he was called Ricky of the Tuft, Ricky being his family name.

Some seven or eight years later the queen of a neighbouring kingdom gave birth to twin daughters. The first one to come into the world was more beautiful than the dawn, and the queen was so overjoyed that it was feared her great excitement might do her some harm. The same fairy who had assisted at the birth of Ricky of the Tuft was present, and, in order to moderate the transports of the queen she declared that this little princess would have no sense at all, and would be as stupid as she was beautiful.

The queen was deeply mortified, and a moment or two later her chagrin became greater still, for the second daughter proved to be extremely ugly.

'Do not be distressed, Madam.' said the fairy; 'your daughter shall be recompensed in another way. She shall have so much good sense that her lack of beauty will scarcely be noticed.'

'May Heaven grant it!' said the queen; 'but is there no means by which the elder, who is so beautiful, can be endowed with some intelligence?'

'In the matter of brains I can do nothing for her, Madam.' said the fairy, 'but as regards beauty I can do a great deal. As there is nothing I would not do to please you, I will bestow upon her the power of making beautiful any person who shall greatly please her.'

As the two princesses grew up their perfections increased, and everywhere the beauty of the elder and the wit of the younger were the subject of common talk.

It is equally true that their defects also increased as they became older. The younger grew uglier every minute, and the elder daily became more stupid. Either she answered nothing at all when spoken to, or replied with some idiotic remark. At the same time she was so awkward that she could not set four china vases on the mantelpiece without breaking one of them, nor drink a glass of water without spilling half of it over her clothes.

Now although the elder girl possessed the great advantage which beauty always confers upon youth, she was nevertheless outshone in almost all company by her younger sister. At first every one gathered round the beauty to see and admire her, but very soon they were all attracted by the graceful and easy conversation of the clever one. In a very short time the elder girl would be left entirely alone, while everybody clustered round her sister.

The elder princess was not so stupid that she was not aware of this, and she would willingly have surrendered all her beauty for half her sister's cleverness. Sometimes she was ready to die of grief, for the queen, though a sensible woman, could not refrain from occasionally reproaching her with her stupidity.

The princess had retired one day to a wood to bemoan her misfortune, when she saw approaching her an ugly little man, of very disagreeable appearance, but clad in magnificent attire.

This was the young prince Ricky of the Tuft. He had fallen in love with her portrait, which was everywhere to be seen, and had left his father's kingdom in order to have the pleasure of seeing and talking to her.

Delighted to meet her thus alone, he approached with every mark of respect and politeness. But while he paid her the usual compliments he noticed that she was plunged in melancholy.

'I cannot understand, madam,' he said, 'how any one with your beauty can be so sad as you appear. I can boast of having seen many fair ladies, and I declare that none of them could compare in beauty with you.'

'It is very kind of you to say so, sir,' answered the princess; and stopped there, at a loss what to say further.

'Beauty,' said Ricky, 'is of such great advantage that everything else can be disregarded; and I do not see that the possessor of it can have anything much to grieve about.'

To this the princess replied:

'I would rather be as plain as you are and have some sense, than be as beautiful as I am and at the same time stupid.'

'Nothing more clearly displays good sense, madam,

than a belief that one is not possessed of it. It follows, therefore, that the more one has, the more one fears it to be wanting.'

'I am not sure about that,' said the princess; 'but I know only too well that I am very stupid, and this is the reason of the misery which is nearly killing me.'

'If that is all that troubles you, madam, I can easily put an end to your suffering.'

'How will you manage that?' said the princess.

'I am able, madam,' said Ricky of the Tuft, 'to bestow as much good sense as it is possible to possess on the person whom I love the most. You are that person, and it therefore rests with you to decide whether you will acquire so much intelligence. The only condition is that you shall consent to marry me.'

The princess was dumbfounded, and remained silent.

'I can see,' pursued Ricky, 'that this suggestion perplexes you, and I am not surprised. But I will give you a whole year to make up your mind to it.'

The princess had so little sense, and at the same time desired it so ardently, that she persuaded herself the end of this year would never come. So she accepted the offer which had been made to her. No sooner had she given her word to Ricky that she would marry him within one year from that very day, than she felt a complete change come over her. She found herself able to say all that she wished with the greatest ease, and to say it in an elegant, finished, and natural manner. She at once engaged Ricky in a brilliant and lengthy conversation, holding her own so well that Ricky feared he had given her a larger share of sense than he had retained for himself.

On her return to the palace amazement reigned throughout the Court at such a sudden and extraordinary change. Whereas formerly they had been accustomed to hear her give vent to silly, pert remarks, they now heard her express herself sensibly and very wittily.

The entire Court was overjoyed. The only person not too pleased was the younger sister, for now that she had no longer the advantage over the elder in wit, she seemed nothing but a little fright in comparison.

The king himself often took her advice, and several times held his councils in her apartment.

The news of this change spread abroad, and the princes of the neighbouring kingdoms made many attempts to captivate her. Almost all asked her in marriage. But she found none with enough sense, and so she listened to all without promising herself to any.

At last came one who was so powerful, so rich, so witty, and so handsome, that she could not help being somewhat attracted by him. Her father noticed this, and told her she could make her own choice of a husband: she had only to declare herself.

Now the more sense one has, the more difficult it is to make up one's mind in an affair of this kind. After thanking her father, therefore, she asked for a little time to think it over.

In order to ponder quietly what she had better do she went to walk in a wood—the very one, as it happened, where she encountered Ricky of the Tuft.

While she walked, deep in thought, she heard beneath her feet a thudding sound, as though many people were running busily to and fro. Listening more attentively she heard voices. 'Bring me that boiler,' said one; then another—'Put some wood on that fire!'

At that moment the ground opened, and she saw below what appeared to be a large kitchen full of cooks and scullions, and all the train of attendants which the preparation of a great banquet involves. A gang of some twenty or thirty spit-turners emerged and took up their positions round a very long table in a path in the wood. They all wore their cook's caps on one side, and with their basting implements in their hands they kept time together as they worked, to the lilt of a melodious song.

The princess was astonished by this spectacle, and asked for whom their work was being done.

'For Prince Ricky of the Tuft, madam,' said the foreman of the gang; 'his wedding is to-morrow.'

At this the princess was more surprised than ever. In a flash she remembered that it was a year to the very day since she had promised to marry Prince Ricky of the Tuft, and was taken aback by the recollection. The reason she had forgotten was that when she made the promise she was still without sense, and with the acquisition of that intelligence which the prince had bestowed upon her, all memory of her former stupidities had been blotted out.

She had not gone another thirty paces when Ricky of the Tuft appeared before her, gallant and resplendent, like a prince upon his wedding day.

'As you see, madam,' he said, 'I keep my word to the minute. I do not doubt that you have come to keep yours, and by giving me your hand to make me the happiest of men.'

'I will be frank with you,' replied the princess. 'I have not yet made up my mind on the point, and I am afraid I shall never be able to take the decision you desire.'

'You astonish me, madam,' said Ricky of the Tuft.

'I can well believe it.' said the princess, 'and undoubtedly, if I had to deal with a clown, or a man who lacked good sense, I should feel myself very awkwardly situated. "A princess must keep her word," he would say, "and you must marry me because you promised to!" But I am speaking to a man of the world, of the greatest good sense, and I am sure that he will listen to reason. As you are aware, I could not make up my mind to marry you even when I was entirely without sense; how can you expect that to-day, possessing the intelligence you bestowed on me, which makes me still more difficult to please than formerly, I should take a decision which I could not take then? If you wished so much to marry me, you were very wrong to relieve me of my stupidity, and to let me see more clearly than I did.'

'If a man who lacked good sense,' replied Ricky of the Tuft, 'would be justified, as you have just said, in reproaching you for breaking your word, why do you expect, madam, that I should act differently where the happiness of my whole life is at stake? Is it reasonable that people who have sense should be treated worse than those who have none? Would you maintain that for a moment—you, who so markedly have sense, and desired so ardently to have it? But, pardon me, let us get to the facts. With the exception of my ugliness, is there anything about me which displeases you? Are you dissatisfied with my breeding, my brains, my disposition, or my manners?'

'In no way,' replied the princess; 'I like exceedingly all that you have displayed of the qualities you mention.'

'In that case,' said Ricky of the Tuft, 'happiness will be mine, for it lies in your power to make me the most attractive of men.'

'How can that be done?' asked the princess.

'It will happen of itself,' replied Ricky of the Tuft, 'if you love me well enough to wish that it be so. To remove your doubts, madam, let me tell you that the same fairy who on the day of my birth bestowed upon me the power of endowing with intelligence the woman of my choice, gave to you also the power of endowing with beauty the man whom you should love, and on whom you should wish to confer this favour.'

'If that is so,' said the princess, 'I wish with all my heart that you may become the handsomest and most attractive prince in the world, and I give you without reserve the boon which it is mine to bestow.'

No sooner had the princess uttered these words than Ricky of the Tuft appeared before her eyes as the handsomest, most graceful and attractive man that she had ever set eyes on.

Some people assert that this was not the work of fairy enchantment, but that love alone brought about the transformation. They say that the princess, as she mused upon her lover's constancy, upon his good sense, and his many admirable qualities of heart and head, grew blind to the deformity of his body and the ugliness of his face; that his hump back seemed no more than was natural in a man who could make the courtliest of bows, and that the dreadful limp which had formerly distressed her now betokened nothing more than a certain diffidence and charming deference of manner. They say further that she found his eyes shine all the brighter for their squint, and that this defect in them was to her but a sign of passionate love; while his great red nose she found nought but martial and heroic.

However that may be, the princess promised to marry him on the spot, provided only that he could obtain the consent of her royal father.

The king knew Ricky of the Tuft to be a prince both wise and witty, and on learning of his daughter's regard for him, he accepted him with pleasure as a son-in-law.

The wedding took place upon the morrow, just as Ricky of the Tuft had foreseen, and in accordance with the arrangements he had long ago put in train.

CINDERELLA, OR THE LITTLE GLASS SLIPPER

Once upon a time there was a worthy man who married for his second wife the haughtiest, proudest woman that had ever been seen. She had two daughters, who possessed their mother's temper and resembled her in everything. Her husband, on the other hand, had a young daughter, who was of an exceptionally sweet and gentle nature. She got this from her mother, who had been the nicest person in the world.

The wedding was no sooner over than the stepmother began to display her bad temper. She could not endure the excellent qualities of this young girl, for they made her own daughters appear more hateful than ever. She thrust upon her all the meanest tasks about the house. It was she who had to clean the plates and the stairs, and sweep out the rooms of the mistress of the house and her daughters. She slept on a wretched mattress in a garret at the top of the house, while the sisters had rooms with parquet flooring, and beds of the most fashionable style, with mirrors in which they could see themselves from top to toe.

The poor girl endured everything patiently, not daring to complain to her father. The latter would have scolded her, because he was entirely ruled by his wife. When she had finished her work she used to sit amongst the cinders in the corner of the chimney, and it was from this habit that she came to be commonly known as Cindertail. The younger of the two sisters, who was not quite so spiteful as the elder, called her Cinderella. But her wretched clothes did not prevent Cinderella from being a hundred times more beautiful than her sisters, for all their resplendent garments.

It happened that the king's son gave a ball, and he invited all persons of high degree. The two young ladies were invited amongst others, for they cut a considerable figure in the country. Not a little pleased were they, and the question of what clothes and what mode of dressing the hair would become them best took up all their time. And all this meant fresh trouble for Cinderella, for it was she who went over her sisters' linen and ironed their ruffles. They could talk of nothing else but the fashions in clothes.

'For my part,' said the elder, 'I shall wear my dress of red velvet, with the Honiton lace.'

'I have only my everyday petticoat,' said the younger, 'but to make up for it I shall wear my cloak with the golden flowers and my necklace of diamonds, which are not so bad.'

They sent for a good hairdresser to arrange their double-frilled caps, and bought patches at the best shop.

They summoned Cinderella and asked her advice, for she had good taste. Cinderella gave them the best possible suggestions, and even offered to dress their hair, to which they gladly agreed.

While she was thus occupied they said:

'Cinderella, would you not like to go to the ball?'

'Ah, but you fine young ladies are laughing at me. It would be no place for me.'

'That is very true, people would laugh to see a cindertail in the ballroom.'

Any one else but Cinderella would have done their hair amiss, but she was good-natured, and she finished them off to perfection. They were so excited in their glee that for nearly two days they ate nothing. They broke more than a dozen laces through drawing their stays tight in order to make their waists more slender, and they were perpetually in front of a mirror.

At last the happy day arrived. Away they went, Cinderella watching them as long as she could keep them in sight. When she could no longer see them she began to cry. Her godmother found her in tears, and asked what was troubling her.

'I should like—I should like—'

She was crying so bitterly that she could not finish the sentence.

Said her godmother, who was a fairy:

'You would like to go to the ball, would you not?'

'Ah, yes,' said Cinderella, sighing.

'Well, well,' said her godmother, 'promise to be a good girl and I will arrange for you to go.'

She took Cinderella into her room and said:

'Go into the garden and bring me a pumpkin.'

Cinderella went at once and gathered the finest that she could find. This she brought to her godmother, wondering how a pumpkin could help in taking her to the ball.

Her godmother scooped it out, and when only the rind was left, struck it with her wand. Instantly the pumpkin was changed into a beautiful coach, gilded all over.

Then she went and looked in the mouse-trap, where she found six mice all alive. She told Cinderella to lift the door of the mouse-trap a little, and as each mouse came out she gave it a tap with her wand, whereupon it was transformed into a fine horse. So that here was a fine team of six dappled mouse-grey horses.

But she was puzzled to know how to provide a coachman.

'I will go and see,' said Cinderella, 'if there is not a rat in the rat-trap. We could make a coachman of him.'

'Quite right,' said her godmother, 'go and see.'

Cinderella brought in the rat-trap, which contained three big rats. The fairy chose one specially on account of his elegant whiskers.

As soon as she had touched him he turned into a fat coachman with the finest moustachios that ever were seen.

'Now go into the garden and bring me the six lizards which you will find behind the water-butt.'

No sooner had they been brought than the godmother turned them into six lackeys, who at once climbed up behind the coach in their braided liveries, and hung on there as if they had never done anything else all their lives.

Then said the fairy godmother:

'Well, there you have the means of going to the ball. Are you satisfied?'

'Oh, yes, but am I to go like this in my ugly clothes?'

Her godmother merely touched her with her wand, and on the instant her clothes were changed into garments of gold and silver cloth, bedecked with jewels. After that her godmother gave her a pair of glass slippers, the prettiest in the world.

Thus altered, she entered the coach. Her godmother bade her not to stay beyond midnight whatever happened, warning her that if she remained at the ball a moment longer, her coach would again become a pumpkin, her horses mice, and her lackeys lizards, while her old clothes would reappear upon her once more.

She promised her godmother that she would not fail to leave the ball before midnight, and away she went, beside herself with delight.

The king's son, when he was told of the arrival of a great princess whom nobody knew, went forth to receive her. He handed her down from the coach, and led her into the hall where the company was assembled. At once there fell a great silence. The dancers stopped, the violins played no more, so rapt was the attention which everybody bestowed upon the superb beauty of the unknown guest. Everywhere could be heard in confused whispers:

'Oh, how beautiful she is!'

The king, old man as he was, could not take his eyes off her, and whispered to the queen that it was many a long day since he had seen any one so beautiful and charming.

All the ladies were eager to scrutinise her clothes and the dressing of her hair, being determined to copy them on the morrow, provided they could find materials so fine, and tailors so clever.

The king's son placed her in the seat of honour, and at once begged the privilege of being her partner in a dance. Such was the grace with which she danced that the admiration of all was increased.

A magnificent supper was served, but the young prince could eat nothing, so taken up was he with watching her. She went and sat beside her sisters, and bestowed numberless attentions upon them. She made them share with her the oranges and lemons which the king had given her—greatly to their astonishment, for they did not recognise her.

While they were talking, Cinderella heard the clock strike a quarter to twelve. She at once made a profound curtsey to the company, and departed as quickly as she could.

As soon as she was home again she sought out her godmother, and having thanked her, declared that she wished to go upon the morrow once more to the ball, because the king's son had invited her.

While she was busy telling her godmother all that had happened at the ball, her two sisters knocked at the door. Cinderella let them in.

'What a long time you have been in coming!' she

declared, rubbing her eyes and stretching herself as if she had only just awakened. In real truth she had not for a moment wished to sleep since they had left.

'If you had been at the ball,' said one of the sisters, 'you would not be feeling weary. There came a most beautiful princess, the most beautiful that has ever been seen, and she bestowed numberless attentions upon us, and gave us her oranges and lemons.'

Cinderella was overjoyed. She asked them the name of the princess, but they replied that no one knew it, and that the king's son was so distressed that he would give anything in the world to know who she was.

Cinderella smiled, and said she must have been beautiful indeed.

'Oh, how lucky you are. Could I not manage to see her? Oh, please, Javotte, lend me the yellow dress which you wear every day.'

'Indeed!' said Javotte, 'that is a fine idea. Lend my dress to a grubby cindertail like you—you must think me mad!'

Cinderella had expected this refusal. She was in no way upset, for she would have been very greatly embarrassed had her sister been willing to lend the dress.

The next day the two sisters went to the ball, and so did Cinderella, even more splendidly attired than the first time.

The king's son was always at her elbow, and paid her endless compliments.

The young girl enjoyed herself so much that she forgot her godmother's bidding completely, and when the first stroke of midnight fell upon her ears, she thought it was no more than eleven o'clock.

She rose and fled as nimbly as a fawn. The prince followed her, but could not catch her. She let fall one of her glass slippers, however, and this the prince picked up with tender care.

When Cinderella reached home she was out of breath, without coach, without lackeys, and in her shabby clothes. Nothing remained of all her splendid clothes save one of the little slippers, the fellow to the one which she had let fall.

Inquiries were made of the palace doorkeepers as to whether they had seen a princess go out, but they declared they had seen no one leave except a young girl, very ill-clad, who looked more like a peasant than a young lady.

When her two sisters returned from the ball, Cinderella asked them if they had again enjoyed themselves, and if the beautiful lady had been there. They told her that she was present, but had fled away when midnight sounded, and in such haste that she had let fall one of her little glass slippers, the prettiest thing in the world. They added that the king's son, who picked it up, had done nothing but gaze at it for the rest of the ball, from which it was plain that he was deeply in love with its beautiful owner.

They spoke the truth. A few days later, the king's son caused a proclamation to be made by trumpeters, that he would take for wife the owner of the foot which the slipper would fit.

They tried it first on the princesses, then on the duchesses and the whole of the Court, but in vain. Presently they brought it to the home of the two sisters, who did all they could to squeeze a foot into the slipper. This, however, they could not manage.

Cinderella was looking on and recognised her slipper:

'Let me see,' she cried, laughingly, 'if it will not fit me.'

Her sisters burst out laughing, and began to gibe at her, but the equerry who was trying on the slipper looked closely at Cinderella. Observing that she was very beautiful he declared that the claim was quite a fair one, and that his orders were to try the slipper on every maiden. He bade Cinderella sit down, and on putting the slipper to her little foot he perceived that the latter slid in without trouble, and was moulded to its shape like wax.

Great was the astonishment of the two sisters at this, and greater still when Cinderella drew from her pocket the other little slipper. This she likewise drew on.

At that very moment her godmother appeared on the scene. She gave a tap with her wand to Cinderella's clothes, and transformed them into a dress even more magnificent than her previous ones.

The two sisters recognised her for the beautiful person whom they had seen at the ball, and threw themselves at her feet, begging her pardon for all the ill-treatment she had suffered at their hands.

Cinderella raised them, and declaring as she embraced them that she pardoned them with all her heart, bade them to love her well in future.

She was taken to the palace of the young prince in all her new array. He found her more beautiful than ever, and was married to her a few days afterwards.

Cinderella was as good as she was beautiful. She set aside apartments in the palace for her two sisters, and married them the very same day to two gentlemen of high rank about the Court.

LITTLE RED RIDING HOOD

Once upon a time there was a little village girl, the prettiest that had ever been seen. Her mother doted on her. Her grand-mother was even fonder, and made her a little red hood, which became her so well that everywhere she went by the name of Little Red Riding Hood.

One day her mother, who had just made and baked some cakes, said to her:

'Go and see how your grandmother is, for I have been told that she is ill. Take her a cake and this little pot of butter.'

Little Red Riding Hood set off at once for the house of her grandmother, who lived in another village.

On her way through a wood she met old Father Wolf. He would have very much liked to eat her, but dared not do so on account of some wood-cutters who were in the forest. He asked her where she was going. The poor child, not knowing that it was dangerous to stop and listen to a wolf, said:

'I am going to see my grandmother, and am taking her a cake and a pot of butter which my mother has sent to her.'

'Does she live far away?' asked the Wolf.

'Oh yes.' replied Little Red Riding Hood; 'it is yonder by the mill which you can see right below there, and it is the first house in the village.'

'Well now,' said the Wolf, 'I think I shall go and see her too. I will go by this path, and you by that path, and we will see who gets there first.'

The Wolf set off running with all his might by the shorter road, and the little girl continued on her way by the longer road. As she went she amused herself by gathering nuts, running after the butterflies, and making nosegays of the wild flowers which she found.

The Wolf was not long in reaching the grandmother's house.

He knocked. *Toc Toc*.

'Who is there?'

'It is your little daughter, Red Riding Hood,' said the Wolf, disguising his voice, 'and I bring you a cake and a little pot of butter as a present from my mother.'

The worthy grandmother was in bed, not being very well, and cried out to him:

'Pull out the peg and the latch will fall.'

The Wolf drew out the peg and the door flew open. Then he sprang upon the poor old lady and ate her up in less than no time, for he had been more than three days without food.

After that he shut the door, lay down in the grandmother's bed, and waited for Little Red Riding Hood.

Presently she came and knocked. *Toc Toc*.

'Who is there?'

Now Little Red Riding Hood on hearing the Wolf's gruff voice was at first frightened, but thinking that her grandmother had a bad cold, she replied:

'It is your little daughter, Red Riding Hood, and I bring you a cake and a little pot of butter from my mother.'

Softening his voice, the Wolf called out to her:

'Pull out the peg and the latch will fall.'

Little Red Riding Hood drew out the peg and the door flew open.

When he saw her enter, the Wolf hid himself in the bed beneath the counterpane.

'Put the cake and the little pot of butter on the bin.' he said, 'and come up on the bed with me.'

Little Red Riding Hood took off her clothes, but when she climbed up on the bed she was astonished to see how her grandmother looked in her nightgown.

'Grandmother dear!' she exclaimed, 'what big arms you have!'

'The better to embrace you, my child!'

'Grandmother dear, what big legs you have!'

'The better to run with, my child!'

'Grandmother dear, what big ears you have!'

'The better to hear with, my child!'

'Grandmother dear, what big eyes you have!'

'The better to see with, my child!'

'Grandmother dear, what big teeth you have!'

'The better to eat you with!'

With these words the wicked Wolf leapt upon Little Red Riding Hood and gobbled her up.

BLUE BEARD

Once upon a time there was a man who owned splendid town and country houses, gold and silver plate, tapestries and coaches gilt all over. But the poor fellow had a blue beard, and this made him so ugly and frightful that there was not a woman or girl who did not run away at sight of him.

Amongst his neighbours was a lady of high degree who had two surpassingly beautiful daughters. He asked for the hand of one of these in marriage, leaving it to their mother to choose which should be bestowed upon him. Both girls, however, raised objections, and his offer was bandied from one to the other, neither being able to bring herself to accept a man with a blue beard. Another reason for their distaste was the fact that he had already married several wives, and no one knew what had become of them.

In order that they might become better acquainted, Blue Beard invited the two girls, with their mother and three or four of their best friends, to meet a party of young men from the neighbourhood at one of his country houses. Here they spent eight whole days, and throughout their stay there was a constant round of picnics, hunting and fishing expeditions, dances, dinners, and luncheons; and they never slept at all, through spending all the night in playing merry pranks upon each other. In short, everything went so gaily that the younger daughter began to think the master of the house had not so very blue a beard after all, and that he was an exceedingly agreeable man. As soon as the party returned to town their marriage took place.

At the end of a month Blue Beard informed his wife that important business obliged him to make a journey into a distant part of the country, which would occupy at least six weeks. He begged her to amuse herself well during his absence, and suggested that she should invite some of her friends and take them, if she liked, to the country. He was particularly anxious that she should enjoy herself thoroughly.

'Here,' he said, 'are the keys of the two large storerooms, and here is the one that locks up the gold and silver plate which is not in everyday use. This key belongs to the strong-boxes where my gold and silver is kept, this to the caskets containing my jewels; while here you have the master-key which gives admittance to all the apartments. As regards this little key, it is the key of the small room at the end of the long passage on the lower floor. You may open everything, you may go everywhere, but I forbid you to enter this little room. And I forbid you so seriously that if you were indeed to open the door, I should be so angry that I might do anything.'

She promised to follow out these instructions exactly, and after embracing her, Blue Beard steps into his coach and is off upon his journey.

Her neighbours and friends did not wait to be invited before coming to call upon the young bride, so great was their eagerness to see the splendours of her house. They had not dared to venture while her husband was there, for his blue beard frightened them. But in less than no time there they were, running in and out of the rooms, the closets, and the wardrobes, each of which was finer than the last.

Presently they went upstairs to the storerooms, and there they could not admire enough the profusion and magnificence of the tapestries, beds, sofas, cabinets, tables, and stands. There were mirrors in which they could view themselves from top to toe, some with frames of plate glass, others with frames of silver and gilt lacquer, that were the most superb and beautiful things that had ever been seen. They were loud and persistent in their envy of their friend's good fortune. She, on the other hand, derived little amusement from the sight of all these riches, the reason being that she was impatient to go and inspect the little room on the lower floor.

So overcome with curiosity was she that, without reflecting upon the discourtesy of leaving her guests, she ran down a private staircase, so precipitately that twice or thrice she nearly broke her neck, and so reached the door of the little room. There she paused for a while, thinking of the prohibition which her husband had made, and reflecting that harm might come to her as a result of disobedience. But the temptation was so great that she could not conquer it. Taking the little key, with a trembling hand she opened the door of the room.

At first she saw nothing, for the windows were closed, but after a few moments she perceived dimly that the floor was entirely covered with clotted blood, and that in this were reflected the dead bodies of several women that hung along the walls. These were all the wives of Blue Beard, whose throats he had cut, one after another.

She thought to die of terror, and the key of the room, which she had just withdrawn from the lock, fell from her hand.

When she had somewhat regained her senses, she picked up the key, closed the door, and went up to her chamber to compose herself a little. But this she could not do, for her nerves were too shaken. Noticing that the key of the little room was stained with blood, she wiped it two or three times. But the blood did not go. She washed it well, and even rubbed it with sand and grit. Always the blood remained. For the key was bewitched, and there was no means of cleaning it completely. When the blood was removed from one side, it reappeared on the other.

Blue Beard returned from his journey that very evening. He had received some letters on the way, he said, from which he learned that the business upon which he had set forth had just been concluded to his satisfaction. His wife did everything she could to make it appear that she was delighted by his speedy return.

On the morrow he demanded the keys. She gave them to him, but with so trembling a hand that he guessed at once what had happened.

'How comes it,' he said to her, 'that the key of the little room is not with the others?'

'I must have left it upstairs upon my table.' she said.

'Do not fail to bring it to me presently.' said Blue Beard.

After several delays the key had to be brought. Blue Beard examined it, and addressed his wife.

'Why is there blood on this key?'

'I do not know at all,' replied the poor woman, paler than death.

'You do not know at all?' exclaimed Blue Beard; 'I know well enough. You wanted to enter the little room! Well, madam, enter it you shall—you shall go and take your place among the ladies you have seen there.'

She threw herself at her husband's feet, asking his pardon with tears, and with all the signs of a true repentance for her disobedience. She would have softened a rock, in her beauty and distress, but Blue Beard had a heart harder than any stone.

'You must die, madam,' he said; 'and at once.'

'Since I must die.' she replied, gazing at him with eyes

that were wet with tears, 'give me a little time to say my prayers.'

'I give you one quarter of an hour,' replied Blue Beard, 'but not a moment longer.'

When the poor girl was alone, she called her sister to her and said:

'Sister Anne'—for that was her name—'go up, I implore you, to the top of the tower, and see if my brothers are not approaching. They promised that they would come and visit me to-day. If you see them, make signs to them to hasten.'

Sister Anne went up to the top of the tower, and the poor unhappy girl cried out to her from time to time:

'Anne, Sister Anne, do you see nothing coming?'

And Sister Anne replied:

'I see nought but dust in the sun and the green grass growing.'

Presently Blue Beard, grasping a great cutlass, cried out at the top of his voice:

'Come down quickly, or I shall come upstairs myself.'

'Oh please, one moment more.' called out his wife.

And at the same moment she cried in a whisper:

'Anne, Sister Anne, do you see nothing coming?'

'I see nought but dust in the sun and the green grass growing.'

'Come down at once, I say.' shouted Blue Beard, 'or I will come upstairs myself.'

'I am coming.' replied his wife.

Then she called:

'Anne, Sister Anne, do you see nothing coming?'

'I see,' replied Sister Anne, 'a great cloud of dust which comes this way.'

'Is it my brothers?'

'Alas, sister, no; it is but a flock of sheep.'

'Do you refuse to come down?' roared Blue Beard.

'One little moment more!' exclaimed his wife.

Once more she cried:

'Anne, Sister Anne, do you see nothing coming?'

'I see,' replied her sister, 'two horsemen who come this way, but they are as yet a long way off. . . Heaven be praised!' she exclaimed a moment later, 'they are my brothers. . . I am signalling to them all I can to hasten.'

Blue Beard let forth so mighty a shout that the whole house shook. The poor wife went down and cast herself at his feet, all dishevelled and in tears.

'That avails you nothing,' said Blue Beard; 'you must die.'

Seizing her by the hair with one hand, and with the other brandishing the cutlass aloft, he made as if to cut off her head.

The poor woman, turning towards him and fixing a dying gaze upon him, begged for a brief moment in which to collect her thoughts.

'No! no!' he cried; 'commend your soul to Heaven.' And raising his arm—

At this very moment there came so loud a knocking at the gate that Blue Beard stopped short. The gate was opened, and two horsemen dashed in, who drew their swords and rode straight at Blue Beard. The latter recognised them as the brothers of his wife—one of them a dragoon, and the other a musketeer—and fled instantly in an effort to escape. But the two brothers were so close upon him that they caught him ere he could gain the first flight of steps. They plunged their swords through his body and left him dead. The poor woman was nearly as dead as her husband, and had not the strength to rise and embrace her brothers.

It was found that Blue Beard had no heirs, and that consequently his wife became mistress of all his wealth. She devoted a portion to arranging a marriage between her sister Anne and a young gentleman with whom the latter had been for some time in love, while another portion purchased a captain's commission for each of her brothers. The rest formed a dowry for her own marriage with a very worthy man, who banished from her mind all memory of the evil days she had spent with Blue Beard.

THE RIDICULOUS WISHES

In days long past there lived a poor woodcutter who found life very hard. Indeed, it was his lot to toil for little guerdon, and although he was young and happily married there were moments when he wished himself dead and below ground.

One day while at his work he was again lamenting his fate.

'Some men,' he said, 'have only to make known their desires, and straightway these are granted, and their every wish fulfilled; but it has availed me little to wish for ought, for the gods are deaf to the prayers of such as I.'

As he spoke these words there was a great noise of thunder, and Jupiter appeared before him wielding his mighty thunderbolts. Our poor man was stricken with fear and threw himself on the ground.

'My lord,' he said, 'forget my foolish speech; heed not my wishes, but cease thy thundering!'

'Have no fear,' answered Jupiter; 'I have heard thy plaint, and have come hither to show thee how greatly thou dost wrong me. Hark! I, who am sovereign lord of this world, promise to grant in full the first three wishes which it will please thee to utter, whatever these may be. Consider well what things can bring thee joy and prosperity, and as thy happiness is at stake, be not over-hasty, but revolve the matter in thy mind.'

Having thus spoken Jupiter withdrew himself and made his ascent to Olympus. As for our woodcutter, he blithely corded his faggot, and throwing it over his shoulder, made for his home. To one so light of heart the load also seemed light, and his thoughts were merry as he strode along. Many a wish came into his mind, but he was resolved to seek the advice of his wife, who was a young woman of good understanding.

He had soon reached his cottage, and casting down his faggot:

'Behold me, Fanny,' he said. 'Make up the fire and spread the board, and let there be no stint. We are wealthy, Fanny, wealthy for evermore; we have only to wish for whatsoever we may desire.'

Thereupon he told her the story of what had befallen that day. Fanny, whose mind was quick and active, immediately conceived many plans for the advancement of their fortune, but she approved her husband's resolve to act with prudence and circumspection.

''Twere a pity,' she said, 'to spoil our chances through impatience. We had best take counsel of the night, and wish no wishes until to-morrow.'

'That is well spoken,' answered Harry. 'Meanwhile fetch a bottle of our best, and we shall drink to our good fortune.'

Fanny brought a bottle from the store behind the faggots, and our man enjoyed his ease, leaning back in his chair with his toes to the fire and his goblet in his hand.

'What fine glowing embers!' he said, 'and what a fine toasting fire! I wish we had a black pudding at hand.'

Hardly had he spoken these words when his wife beheld, to her great astonishment, a long black pudding which, issuing from a corner of the hearth, came winding and wriggling towards her. She uttered a cry of fear, and then again exclaimed in dismay, when she perceived that this strange occurrence was due to the wish which her husband had so rashly and foolishly spoken. Turning upon him, in her anger and disappointment she called the poor man all the abusive names that she could think of.

'What!' she said to him, 'when you can call for a kingdom, for gold, pearls, rubies, diamonds, for princely garments and wealth untold, is this the time to set your mind upon black puddings!'

'Nay!' answered the man, ''twas a thoughtless speech, and a sad mistake; but I shall now be on my guard, and shall do better next time.'

'Who knows that you will?' returned his wife. 'Once a witless fool, always a witless fool!' and giving free rein to her vexation and ill-temper she continued to upbraid her husband until his anger also was stirred, and he had well-nigh made a second bid and wished himself a widower.

'Enough! woman,' he cried at last; 'put a check upon thy froward tongue! Who ever heard such impertinence as this! A plague on the shrew and on her pudding! Would to heaven it hung at the end of her nose!'

No sooner had the husband given voice to these words than the wish was straightway granted, and the long coil of black pudding appeared grafted to the angry dame's nose.

Our man paused when he beheld what he had wrought. Fanny was a comely young woman, and blest with good looks, and truth to tell, this new ornament did not set off her beauty. Yet it offered one advantage, that as it hung right before her mouth, it would thus effectively curb her speech.

So, having now but one wish left, he had all but resolved to make good use of it without further delay, and, before any other mischance could befall, to wish himself a kingdom of his own. He was about to speak the word, when he was stayed by a sudden thought.

'It is true,' he said to himself, 'that there is none so great as a King, but what of the Queen that must share his dignity? With what grace would she sit beside me on the throne with a yard of black pudding for a nose?'

In this dilemma he resolved to put the case to Fanny, and to leave her to decide whether she would rather be a Queen, with this most horrible appendage marring her good looks, or remain a peasant wife, but with her shapely nose relieved of this untoward addition.

Fanny's mind was soon made up: although she had dreamt of a crown and sceptre, yet a woman's first wish is always to please. To this great desire all else must yield, and Fanny would rather be fair in drugget than be a Queen with an ugly face.

Thus our woodcutter did not change his state, did not become a potentate, nor fill his purse with golden crowns. He was thankful enough to use his remaining wish to a more humble purpose, and forthwith relieved his wife of her encumbrance.

The Moral
Ah! so it is that miserable man,
By nature fickle, blind, unwise, and rash,
Oft fails to reap a harvest from great gifts
Bestowed upon him by the heav'nly gods.

DONKEY-SKIN

Once upon a time there was a King, so great, so beloved by his people, and so respected by all his neighbours and allies that one might almost say he was the happiest monarch alive. His good fortune was made even greater by the choice he had made for wife of a Princess as beautiful as she was virtuous, with whom he lived in perfect happiness. Now, of this chaste marriage was born a daughter endowed with so many gifts that they had no regret because other children were not given to them.

Magnificence, good taste, and abundance reigned in the palace; there were wise and clever ministers, virtuous and devoted courtiers, faithful and diligent servants. The spacious stables were filled with the most beautiful horses in the world, and coverts of rich caparison; but what most astonished strangers who came to admire them was to see, in the finest stall, a master donkey, with great long ears.

Now, it was not for a whim but for a good reason that the King had given this donkey a particular and distinguished place. The special qualities of this rare animal deserved the distinction, since nature had made it in so extraordinary a way that its litter, instead of being like that of other donkeys, was covered every morning with an abundance of beautiful golden crowns, and golden louis of every kind, which were collected daily.

Since the vicissitudes of life wait on Kings as much as on their subjects, and good is always mingled with ill, it so befell that the Queen was suddenly attacked by a fatal illness, and, in spite of science, and the skill of the doctors, no remedy could be found. There was great mourning throughout the land. The King who, notwithstanding the famous proverb, that marriage is the tomb of love, was deeply attached to his wife, was distressed beyond measure and made fervent vows to all the temples in his kingdom, and offered to give his life for that of his beloved consort; but he invoked the gods and the Fairies in vain. The Queen, feeling her last hour approach, said to her husband, who was dissolved in tears: 'It is well that I should speak to you of a certain matter before I die: if, perchance, you should desire to marry again. . . .' At these words the King broke into piteous cries, took his wife's hands in his own, and assured her that it was useless to speak to him of a second marriage.

'No, my dear spouse,' he said at last, 'speak to me rather of how I may follow you.'

'The State,' continued the Queen with a finality which but increased the laments of the King, 'the State demands successors, and since I have only given you a daughter, it will urge you to beget sons who resemble you; but I ask you earnestly not to give way to the persuasions of your people until you have found a Princess more beautiful and more perfectly fashioned than I. I beg you to swear this to me, and then I shall die content.'

Perchance, the Queen, who did not lack self-esteem, exacted this oath firmly believing that there was not her equal in the world, and so felt assured that the King would never marry again. Be this as it may, at length she died, and never did husband make so much lamentation; the King wept and sobbed day and night, and the punctilious fulfilment of the rites of widower-hood, even the smallest, was his sole occupation.

But even great griefs do not last for ever. After a time the magnates of the State assembled and came to the King, urging him to take another wife. At first this request seemed hard to him and made him shed fresh tears. He pleaded the vows he had made to the Queen, and defied his counsellors to find a Princess more beautiful and better fashioned than was she, thinking this to be impossible. But the Council treated the promise as a trifle, and said that it mattered little about beauty if the Queen were but virtuous and fruitful. For the State needed Princes for its peace and prosperity, and though, in truth, the Princess, his daughter, had all the qualities requisite for making a great Queen, yet of necessity she must choose an alien for her husband, and then the stranger would take her away with him. If, on the other hand, he remained in her country and shared the throne with her, their children would not be considered to be of pure native stock, and so, there being no Prince of his name, neighbouring peoples would stir up wars, and the kingdom would be ruined.

The King, impressed by these considerations, promised that he would think over the matter. And so search was made among all the marriageable Princesses for one that would suit him. Every day charming portraits were brought him, but none gave promise of the beauty of his late Queen; instead of coming to a decision he brooded over his sorrow until in the end his reason left him. In his delusions he imagined himself once more a young man; he thought the Princess his daughter, in her youth and beauty, was his Queen as he had known her in the days of their courtship, and living thus in the past he urged the unhappy girl to speedily become his bride.

The young Princess, who was virtuous and chaste, threw herself at the feet of the King her father and conjured him, with all the eloquence she could command, not to constrain her to consent to his unnatural desire.

The King, in his madness, could not understand the reason of her desperate reluctance, and asked an old Druid-priest to set the conscience of the Princess at rest. Now this Druid, less religious than ambitious, sacrificed the cause of innocence and virtue to the favour of so great a monarch, and instead of trying to restore the King to his right mind, he encouraged him in his delusion.

The young Princess, beside herself with misery, at last bethought her of the Lilac-fairy, her godmother; determined to consult her, she set out that same night in a pretty little carriage drawn by a great sheep who knew all the roads. When she arrived the Fairy, who loved the Princess, told her that she knew all she had come to say, but that she need have no fear, for nothing would harm her if only she faithfully fulfilled the Fairy's injunctions. 'For, my dear child,' she said to her, 'it would be a great sin to submit to your father's wishes, but you can avoid the necessity without displeasing him. Tell him that to satisfy a whim you have, he must give you a dress the colour of the weather. Never, in spite of all his love and his power will he be able to give you that.'

The Princess thanked her godmother from her heart, and the next morning spoke to the King as the Fairy had counselled her, and protested that no one would win her hand unless he gave her a dress the colour of the weather. The King, overjoyed and hopeful, called together the most skilful workmen, and demanded this robe of them; otherwise they should be hanged. But he was saved from resorting to this extreme measure, since, on the second day, they brought the much desired robe. The heavens are not a more beautiful blue, when they are girdled with clouds of gold, than was that lovely dress when it was unfolded. The Princess was very sad because of it, and did not know what to do.

Once more she went to her Fairy-godmother who, astonished that her plan had been foiled, now told her to ask for another gown the colour of the moon.

The King again sought out the most clever workmen and expressly commanded them to make a dress the colour of the moon; and woe betide them if between the giving of the order and the bringing of the dress more than twenty-four hours should elapse.

The Princess, though pleased with the dress when it was delivered, gave way to distress when she was with her women and her nurse. The Lilac-fairy, who knew all, hastened to comfort her and said: 'Either I am greatly deceived or it is certain that if you ask for a dress the colour of the sun we shall at last baffle the King your father, for it would never be possible to make such a gown; in any case we should gain time.'

So the Princess asked for yet another gown as the Fairy bade her. The infatuated King could refuse his daughter nothing, and he gave without regret all the diamonds and rubies in his crown to aid this superb work; nothing was to be spared that could make the dress as beautiful as the sun. And, indeed, when the dress appeared, all those who unfolded it were obliged to close their eyes, so much were they dazzled. And, truth to tell, green spectacles and smoked glasses date from that time.

What was the Princess to do? Never had so beautiful and so artistic a robe been seen. She was dumb-founded, and pretending that its brilliance had hurt her eyes she retired to her chamber, where she found the Fairy awaiting her.

On seeing the dress like the sun, the Lilac-fairy became red with rage. 'Oh! this time, my child,' she said to the Princess, 'we will put the King to terrible proof. In spite of his madness I think he will be a little astonished by the request that I counsel you to make of him; it is that he should give you the skin of that ass he loves so dearly, and which supplies him so profusely with the means of paying all his expenses. Go, and do not fail to tell him that you want this skin.' The Princess, overjoyed at finding yet another avenue of escape; for she thought that her father could never bring himself to sacrifice the ass, went to find him, and unfolded to him her latest desire.

Although the King was astonished by this whim, he did not hesitate to satisfy it; the poor ass was sacrificed and the skin brought, with due ceremony, to the Princess, who, seeing no other way of avoiding her ill-fortune, was desperate.

At that moment her godmother arrived. 'What are you doing, my child?' she asked, seeing the Princess tearing her hair, her beautiful cheeks stained with tears. 'This is the most happy moment of your life. Wrap yourself in this skin, leave the palace, and walk so long as you can find ground to carry you: when one sacrifices everything to virtue the gods know how to mete out reward. Go, and I will take care that your possessions follow you; in whatever place you rest, your chest with your clothes and your jewels will follow your steps, and here is my wand which I will give you: tap the ground with it when you have need of the chest, and it will appear before your eyes: but haste to set forth, and do not delay.' The Princess embraced her godmother many times, and begged her not to forsake her. Then after she had smeared herself with soot from the chimney, she wrapped herself up in that ugly skin and went out from the magnificent palace without being recognised by a single person.

The absence of the Princess caused a great commotion. The King, who had caused a sumptuous banquet to be prepared, was inconsolable. He sent out more than a hundred gendarmes, and more than a thousand musketeers in quest of her; but the Lilac-fairy made her invisible to the cleverest seekers, and thus she escaped their vigilance.

Meanwhile the Princess walked far, far and even farther away; after a time she sought for a resting place, but although out of charity people gave her food, she was so dishevelled and dirty that no one wanted to keep her. At length she came to a beautiful town, at the gate of which was a small farm. Now the farmer's wife had need of a wench to wash the dishes and to attend to the geese and the pigs, and seeing so dirty a vagrant offered to engage her. The Princess, who was now much fatigued, accepted joyfully. She was put into a recess in the kitchen where for the first days she was subjected to the coarse jokes of the men-servants, so dirty and unpleasant did the donkey-skin make her appear. At last they tired of their pleasantries; moreover she was so attentive to her work that the farmer's wife took her under her protection. She minded the sheep, and penned them up when it was necessary, and she took the geese out to feed with such intelligence that it seemed as if she had never done anything else. Everything that her beautiful hands undertook was done well.

One day she was sitting near a clear fountain where she often repaired to bemoan her sad condition, when she thought she would look at herself in the water. The horrible donkey-skin which covered her from head to toe revolted her. Ashamed, she washed her face and her hands, which became whiter than ivory, and once again her lovely complexion took its natural freshness. The joy of finding herself so beautiful filled her with the desire to bathe in the pool, and this she did. But she had to don her unworthy skin again before she returned to the farm.

By good fortune the next day chanced to be a holiday, and so she had leisure to tap for her chest with the fairy's wand, arrange her toilet, powder her beautiful hair and put on the lovely gown which was the colour of the weather; but the room was so small that the train could not be properly spread out. The beautiful Princess looked at herself, and with good reason, admired her appearance so much that she resolved to wear her magnificent dresses in turn on holidays and Sundays for her own amusement, and this she regularly did. She entwined flowers and diamonds in her lovely hair with admirable art, and often she sighed that she had no witness of her beauty save the sheep and geese, who loved her just as much in the horrible donkey-skin after which she had been named at the farm.

One holiday when Donkey-skin had put on her sun-hued dress, the son of the King to whom the farm belonged alighted there to rest on his return from the hunt. This Prince was young and handsome, beloved of his father and of the Queen his mother, and adored by the people. After he had partaken of the simple collation which was offered him he set out to inspect the farm-yard and all its nooks and corners. In going thus from place to place, he entered a dark alley at the bottom of which was a closed door. Curiosity made him put his eye to the keyhole. Imagine his astonishment at seeing a Princess so beautiful and so richly dressed, and withal of so noble and dignified a mien, that he took her to be a divinity. The impetuosity of his feelings at this moment would have made him force the door, had it not been for the respect with which that charming figure filled him.

It was with difficulty that he withdrew from this gloomy little alley, intent on discovering who the inmate of the tiny room might be. He was told that it was a scullion called Donkey-skin because of the skin which she always wore, and that she was so dirty and unpleasant that no one took any notice of her, or even spoke to her; she had just been taken out of pity to look after the geese.

The Prince, though little satisfied by this information, saw that these dense people knew no more, and that it was useless to question them. So he returned to the palace of the King his father, beyond words in love, having continually before his eyes the beautiful image of the goddess whom he had seen through the keyhole. He was full of regret that he had not knocked at the door, and promised himself that he would not fail to do so next time. But the fervency of his love caused him such great agitation that the same night he was seized by a terrible fever, and was soon at death's door. The Queen, who had no other child, was in despair because all remedies proved useless. In vain she promised great rewards to the doctors; though they exerted all their skill, nothing would cure the Prince. At last they decided that some great sorrow had caused this terrible fever. They told the Queen, who, full of tenderness for her son, went to him and begged him to tell her his trouble. She declared that even if it was a matter of giving him the crown, his father would yield the throne to him without regret; or if he desired some Princess, even though there should be war with the King her father and their subjects should, with reason, complain, all should be sacrificed to obtain what he wished. She implored him with tears not to die, since their life depended on his. The Queen did not finish this touching discourse without moving the Prince to tears.

'Madam,' he said at last, in a very feeble voice, 'I am not so base that I desire the crown of my father, rather may Heaven grant him life for many years, and that I may always be the most faithful and the most respectful of his subjects! As to the Princesses that you speak of, I have never yet thought of marriage, and you well know that, subject as I am to your wishes, I shall obey you always, even though it be painful to me.'

'Ah! my son,' replied the Queen, 'we will spare nothing to save your life. But, my dear child, save mine and that of the King your father by telling me what you desire, and be assured that you shall have it.'

'Well, Madam,' he said, 'since you would have me tell you my thought, I obey you. It would indeed be a sin to place in danger two lives so dear to me. Know, my mother, that I wish Donkey-skin to make me a cake, and to have it brought to me when it is ready.'

The Queen, astonished at this strange name, asked who Donkey-skin might be.

'It is, Madam,' replied one of her officers who had by chance seen this girl, 'It is the most ugly creature imaginable after the wolf, a slut who lodges at your farm, and minds your geese.'

'It matters not,' said the Queen; 'my son, on his way home from the chase, has perchance eaten of her cakes; it is a whim such as those who are sick do sometimes have. In a word, I wish that Donkey-skin, since Donkey-skin it is, make him presently a cake.'

A messenger ran to the farm and told Donkey-skin that she was to make a cake for the Prince as well as she possibly could. Now, some believe that Donkey-skin had been aware of the Prince in her heart at the moment when he had put his eye to the keyhole; and then, looking from her little window, she had seen him, so young, so handsome, and so shapely, that the remembrance of him had remained, and that often the thought of him had cost her some sighs. Be that as it may, Donkey-skin, either having seen him, or having heard him spoken of with praise, was overjoyed to think that she might become known to him. She shut herself in her little room, threw off the ugly skin, bathed her face and hands, arranged her hair, put on a beautiful corsage of bright silver, and an equally beautiful petticoat, and then set herself to make the much desired cake. She took the finest flour, and newest eggs and freshest butter, and while she was working them, whether by design or no, a ring which she had on her finger fell into the cake and was mixed in it. When the cooking was done she muffled herself in her horrible skin and gave the cake to the messenger, asking him for news of the Prince; but the man would not deign to reply, and without a word ran quickly back to the palace.

The Prince took the cake greedily from the man's hands, and ate it with such voracity that the doctors who were present did not fail to say that this haste was not a good sign. Indeed, the Prince came near to being choked by the ring, which he nearly swallowed, in one of the pieces of cake. But he drew it cleverly from his mouth, and his desire for the cake was forgotten as he examined the fine emerald set in a gold keeper-ring, a ring so small that he knew it could only be worn on the prettiest little finger in the world.

He kissed the ring a thousand times, put it under his pillow, and drew it out every moment that he thought himself unobserved. The torment that he gave himself, planning how he might see her to whom the ring belonged, not daring to believe that if he asked for Donkey-skin she would be allowed to come, and not daring to speak of what he had seen through the keyhole for fear that he would be laughed at for a dreamer, brought back the fever with great violence. The doctors, not knowing what more to do, declared to the Queen that the Prince's malady was love, whereupon the Queen and the disconsolate King ran to their son.

'My son, my dear son,' cried the affected monarch, 'tell us the name of her whom you desire: we swear that we will give her to you. Even though she were the vilest of slaves.'

The Queen embracing him, agreed with all that the King had said, and the Prince, moved by their tears and caresses, said to them: 'My father and my mother, I in no way desire to make a marriage which is displeasing to you.' And drawing the emerald from under his pillow he added: 'To prove the truth of this, I desire to marry her to whom this ring belongs. It is not likely that she who owns so pretty a ring is a rustic or a peasant.'

The King and the Queen took the ring, examined it with great curiosity, and agreed with the Prince that it could only belong to the daughter of a good house. Then the King, having embraced his son, and entreated him to get well, went out. He ordered the drums and fifes and trumpets to be sounded throughout the town, and the heralds to cry that she whose finger a certain ring would fit should marry the heir to the throne.

First the Princesses arrived, then the duchesses, and the marquises, and the baronesses; but though they did all they could to make their fingers small, none could put on the ring. So the country girls had to be tried, but pretty though they all were, they all had fingers that were too fat. The Prince, who was feeling better, made the trial himself. At last it was the turn of the chamber-maids; but they succeeded no better. Then, when everyone else had tried, the Prince asked for the kitchen-maids, the scullions, and the sheep-girls. They were all brought to the palace, but their coarse red, short, fingers would hardly go through the golden hoop as far as the nail.

'You have not brought that Donkey-skin, who made me the cake,' said the Prince.

Everyone laughed and said, 'No,' so dirty and unpleasant was she.

'Let someone fetch her at once,' said the King; 'it shall not be said that I left out the lowliest.' And the servants ran laughing and mocking to find the goose-girl.

The Princess, who had heard the drums and the cries of the heralds, had no doubt that the ring was the cause of this uproar. Now, she loved the Prince, and, as true love is timorous and has no vanity, she was in perpetual fear that some other lady would be found to have a finger as small as hers. Great, then, was her joy when the messengers came and knocked at her door. Since she knew that they were seeking the owner of the right finger on which to set her ring, some impulse had moved her to arrange her hair with great care, and to put on her beautiful silver corsage, and the petticoat full of furbelows and silver lace studded with emeralds. At the first knock she quickly covered her finery with the donkey-skin and opened the door. The visitors, in derision, told her that the King had sent for her in order to marry her to his son. Then with loud peals of laughter they led her to the Prince, who was astonished at the garb of this girl, and dared not believe that it was she whom he had seen so majestic and so beautiful. Sad and confounded, he said, 'Is it you who lodge at the bottom of that dark alley in the third yard of the farm?'

'Yes, your Highness,' she replied.

'Show me your hand,' said the Prince trembling, and heaving a deep sigh.

Imagine how astonished everyone was! The King and the Queen, the chamberlains and all the courtiers were dumb-founded, when from beneath that black and dirty skin came a delicate little white and rose-pink hand, and the ring slipped without difficulty on to the prettiest little finger in the world. Then, by a little movement which the Princess made, the skin fell from her shoulders and so enchanting was her guise, that the Prince, weak though he was, fell on his knees and held her so closely that she blushed. But that was scarcely noticed, for the King and Queen came to embrace her heartily, and to ask her if she would marry their son. The Princess, confused by all these caresses and by the love of the handsome young Prince, was about to thank them when suddenly the ceiling opened, and the Lilac-fairy descended in a chariot made of the branches and flowers from which she took her name, and, with great charm, told the Princess's story. The King and Queen, overjoyed to know that Donkey-skin was a great Princess redoubled their caresses, but the Prince was even more sensible of her virtue, and his love increased as the

Fairy unfolded her tale. His impatience to marry her, indeed, was so great that he could scarcely allow time for the necessary preparations for the grand wedding which was their due. The King and Queen, now entirely devoted to their daughter-in-law, overwhelmed her with affection. She had declared that she could not marry the Prince without the consent of the King her father, so, he was the first to whom an invitation to the wedding was sent; he was not, however, told the name of the bride. The Lilac-fairy, who, as was right, presided over all, had recommended this course to prevent trouble. Kings came from all the countries round, some in sedan-chairs, others in beautiful carriages; those who came from the most distant countries rode on elephants and tigers and eagles. But the most magnificent and most glorious of all was the father of the Princess. He had happily recovered his reason, and had married a Queen who was a widow and very beautiful, but by whom he had no child. The Princess ran to him, and he recognised her at once and embraced her with great tenderness before she had time to throw herself on her knees. The King and Queen presented their son to him, and the happiness of all was complete. The nuptials were celebrated with all imaginable pomp, but the young couple were hardly aware of the ceremony, so wrapped up were they in one another.

In spite of the protests of the noble-hearted young man, the Prince's father caused his son to be crowned the same day, and kissing his hand, placed him on the throne.

The celebrations of this illustrious marriage lasted nearly three months, but the love of the two young people would have endured for more than a hundred years, had they out-lived that age, so great was their affection for one another.

The Moral

It scarce may be believed,
This tale of Donkey-skin;
But laughing children in the home,
Yea, mothers, and grandmothers too,
Are little moved by facts!
By them 'twill be received.

CLASSIC LITERATURE: WORDS AND PHRASES
adapted from the Collins English Dictionary

Accoucheur NOUN a male midwife or doctor ❏ *I think my sister must have had some general idea that I was a young offender whom an Accoucheur Policemen had taken up (on my birthday) and delivered over to her* (*Great Expectations* by Charles Dickens)

addled ADJ confused and unable to think properly ❏ *But she counted and counted till she got that addled* (*The Adventures of Huckleberry Finn* by Mark Twain)

admiration NOUN amazement or wonder ❏ *lifting up his hands and eyes by way of admiration* (*Gulliver's Travels* by Jonathan Swift)

afeard ADJ afeard means afraid ❏ *shake it—and don't be afeard* (*The Adventures of Huckleberry Finn* by Mark Twain)

affected VERB affected means to assume the appearance of ❏ *Hadst thou affected sweet divinity* (*Doctor Faustus 5.2* by Christopher Marlowe)

aground ADV when a boat runs aground, it touches the ground in a shallow part of the water and gets stuck ❏ *what kep' you?–boat get aground?* (*The Adventures of Huckleberry Finn* by Mark Twain)

ague NOUN a fever in which the patient has alternate hot and cold shivering fits ❏ *his exposure to the wet and cold had brought on fever and ague* (*Oliver Twist* by Charles Dickens)

alchemy ADJ false or worthless ❏ *all wealth alchemy* (*The Sun Rising* by John Donne)

all alike PHRASE the same all the time ❏ *Love, all alike* (*The Sun Rising* by John Donne)

alow and aloft PHRASE alow means in the lower part or bottom, and aloft means on the top, so alow and aloft means on the top and in the bottom or throughout ❏ *Someone's turned the chest out alow and aloft* (*Treasure Island* by Robert Louis Stevenson)

ambuscade NOUN ambuscade is not a proper word. Tom means an ambush, which is when a group of people attack their enemies, after hiding and waiting for them ❏ *and so we would lie in ambuscade, as he called it* (*The Adventures of Huckleberry Finn* by Mark Twain)

amiable ADJ likeable or pleasant ❏ *Such amiable qualities must speak for themselves* (*Pride and Prejudice* by Jane Austen)

amulet NOUN an amulet is a charm thought to drive away evil spirits. ❏ *uttered phrases at once occult and familiar, like the amulet worn on the heart* (*Silas Marner* by George Eliot)

amusement NOUN here amusement means a strange and disturbing puzzle ❏ *this was an amusement the other way* (*Robinson Crusoe* by Daniel Defoe)

ancient NOUN an ancient was the flag displayed on a ship to show which country it belongs to. It is also called the ensign ❏ *her ancient and pendants out* (*Robinson Crusoe* by Daniel Defoe)

antic ADJ here antic means horrible or grotesque ❏ *armed and dressed after a very antic manner* (*Gulliver's Travels* by Jonathan Swift)

antics NOUN antics is an old word meaning clowns, or people who do silly things to make other people laugh ❏ *And point like antics at his triple crown* (*Doctor Faustus 3.2* by Christopher Marlowe)

appanage NOUN an appanage is a living allowance ❏ *As if loveliness were not the special prerogative of woman–her legitimate appanage and heritage!* (*Jane Eyre* by Charlotte Brontë)

appended VERB appended means attached or added to ❏ *and these words appended* (*Treasure Island* by Robert Louis Stevenson)

approver NOUN an approver is someone who gives evidence against someone he used to work with ❏ *Mr. Noah Claypole: receiving a free pardon from the Crown in consequence of being admitted approver against Fagin* (*Oliver Twist* by Charles Dickens)

areas NOUN the areas is the space, below street level, in front of the basement of a house ❏ *The Dodger had a vicious propensity, too, of pulling the caps from the heads of small boys and tossing them down areas* (*Oliver Twist* by Charles Dickens)

argument NOUN theme or important idea or subject which runs through a piece of writing ❏ *Thrice needful to the argument which now* (*The Prelude* by William Wordsworth)

artificially ADV artfully or cleverly ❏ *and he with a sharp flint sharpened very artificially* (*Gulliver's Travels* by Jonathan Swift)

artist NOUN here artist means a skilled workman ❏ *This man was a most ingenious artist* (*Gulliver's Travels* by Jonathan Swift)

assizes NOUN assizes were regular court sessions which a visiting judge was in charge of ❏ *you shall hang at the next assizes* (*Treasure Island* by Robert Louis Stevenson)

attraction NOUN gravitation, or Newton's theory of gravitation ❏ *he predicted the same fate to attraction* (*Gulliver's Travels* by Jonathan Swift)

aver VERB to aver is to claim something strongly ❏ *for Jem Rodney, the mole catcher, averred that one evening as he was returning homeward* (*Silas Marner* by George Eliot)

baby NOUN here baby means doll, which is a child's toy that looks like a small person ❏ *and skilful dressing her baby* (*Gulliver's Travels* by Jonathan Swift)

bagatelle NOUN bagatelle is a game rather like billiards and pool ❏ *Breakfast had been ordered at a pleasant little tavern, a mile or so away upon the rising ground beyond the green; and there was a bagatelle board in the room, in case we should desire to unbend our minds after the solemnity.* (*Great Expectations* by Charles Dickens)

bah EXCLAM Bah is an exclamation of frustration or anger ❏ *'Bah,' said Scrooge.* (*A Christmas Carol* by Charles Dickens)

bairn NOUN a northern word for child ❏ *Who has taught you those fine words, my bairn?* (*Wuthering Heights* by Emily Brontë)

bait VERB to bait means to stop on a journey to take refreshment ❏ *So, when they stopped to bait the horse, and ate and drank and enjoyed themselves, I could touch nothing that they touched, but kept my fast unbroken.* (*David Copperfield* by Charles Dickens)

balustrade NOUN a balustrade is a row of vertical columns that form railings ❏ *but I mean to say you might have got a hearse up that staircase, and taken it broadwise, with the splinter-bar towards the wall, and the door towards the balustrades: and done it easy* (*A Christmas Carol* by Charles Dickens)

bandbox NOUN a large lightweight box for carrying bonnets or hats ❏ *I am glad I bought my bonnet, if it is only for the fun of having another bandbox* (*Pride and Prejudice* by Jane Austen)

barren NOUN a barren here is a stretch or expanse of barren land ❏ *a line of upright stones, continued the* *length of the barren* (*Wuthering Heights* by Emily Brontë)

basin NOUN a basin was a cup without a handle ❑ *who is drinking his tea out of a basin* (*Wuthering Heights* by Emily Brontë)

battalia NOUN the order of battle ❑ *till I saw part of his army in battalia* (*Gulliver's Travels* by Jonathan Swift)

battery NOUN a Battery is a fort or a place where guns are positioned ❑ *You bring the lot to me, at that old Battery over yonder* (*Great Expectations* by Charles Dickens)

battledore and shuttlecock NOUN The game battledore and shuttlecock was an early version of the game now known as badminton. The aim of the early game was simply to keep the shuttlecock from hitting the ground. ❑ *Battledore and shuttlecock's a wery good game vhen you an't the shuttlecock and two lawyers the battledores, in which case it gets too excitin' to be pleasant* (*Pickwick Papers* by Charles Dickens)

beadle NOUN a beadle was a local official who had power over the poor ❑ *But these impertinences were speedily checked by the evidence of the surgeon, and the testimony of the beadle* (*Oliver Twist* by Charles Dickens)

bearings NOUN the bearings of a place are the measurements or directions that are used to find or locate it ❑ *the bearings of the island* (*Treasure Island* by Robert Louis Stevenson)

beaufet NOUN a beaufet was a sideboard ❑ *and sweet-cake from the beaufet* (*Emma* by Jane Austen)

beck NOUN a beck is a small stream ❑ *a beck which follows the bend of the glen* (*Wuthering Heights* by Emily Brontë)

bedight VERB decorated ❑ *and bedight with Christmas holly stuck into the top.* (*A Christmas Carol* by Charles Dickens)

Bedlam NOUN Bedlam was a lunatic asylum in London which had statues carved by Caius Gabriel Cibber at its entrance ❑ *Bedlam, and those carved maniacs at the gates* (*The Prelude* by William Wordsworth)

beeves NOUN oxen or castrated bulls which are animals used for pulling vehicles or carrying things ❑ *to deliver in every morning six beeves* (*Gulliver's Travels* by Jonathan Swift)

begot VERB created or caused ❑ *Begot in thee* (*On His Mistress* by John Donne)

behoof NOUN behoof means benefit ❑ *'Yes, young man,' said he, releasing the handle of the article in question, retiring a step or two from my table, and speaking for the behoof of the landlord and waiter at the door* (*Great Expectations* by Charles Dickens)

berth NOUN a berth is a bed on a boat ❑ *this is the berth for me* (*Treasure Island* by Robert Louis Stevenson)

bevers NOUN a bever was a snack, or small portion of food, eaten between main meals ❑ *that buys me thirty meals a day and ten bevers* (*Doctor Faustus 2.1* by Christopher Marlowe)

bilge water NOUN the bilge is the widest part of a ship's bottom, and the bilge water is the dirty water that collects there ❑ *no gush of bilge-water had turned it to fetid puddle* (*Jane Eyre* by Charlotte Brontë)

bills NOUN bills is an old term meaning prescription. A prescription is the piece of paper on which your doctor writes an order for medicine and which you give to a chemist to get the medicine ❑ *Are not thy bills hung up as monuments* (*Doctor Faustus 1.1* by Christopher Marlowe)

black cap NOUN a judge wore a black cap when he was about to sentence a prisoner to death ❑ *The judge assumed the black cap, and the prisoner still stood with the same air and gesture.* (*Oliver Twist* by Charles Dickens)

boot-jack NOUN a wooden device to help take boots off ❑ *The speaker appeared to throw a boot-jack, or some such article, at the person he addressed* (*Oliver Twist* by Charles Dickens)

booty NOUN booty means treasure or prizes ❑ *would be inclined to give up their booty in payment of the dead man's debts* (*Treasure Island* by Robert Louis Stevenson)

Bow Street runner PHRASE Bow Street runners were the first British police force, set up by the author Henry Fielding in the eighteenth century ❑ *as would have convinced a judge or a Bow Street runner* (*Treasure Island* by Robert Louis Stevenson)

brawn NOUN brawn is a dish of meat which is set in jelly ❑ *Heaped up upon the floor, to form a kind of throne, were turkeys, geese, game, poultry, brawn, great joints of meat, suckling-pigs* (*A Christmas Carol* by Charles Dickens)

bray VERB when a donkey brays, it makes a loud, harsh sound ❑ *and she doesn't bray like a jackass* (*The Adventures of Huckleberry Finn* by Mark Twain)

break VERB in order to train a horse you first have to break it ❑ *'If a high-mettled creature like this,' said he, 'can't be broken by fair means, she will never be good for anything'* (*Black Beauty* by Anna Sewell)

bullyragging VERB bullyragging is an old word which means bullying. To bullyrag someone is to threaten or force someone to do something they don't want to do ❑ *and a lot of loafers bullyragging him for sport* (*The Adventures of Huckleberry Finn* by Mark Twain)

but PREP except for (this) ❑ *but this, all pleasures fancies be* (*The Good-Morrow* by John Donne)

by hand PHRASE by hand was a common expression of the time meaning that baby had been fed either using a spoon or a bottle rather than by breast-feeding ❑ *My sister, Mrs. Joe Gargery, was more than twenty years older than I, and had established a great reputation with herself . . . because she had bought me up 'by hand'* (*Great Expectations* by Charles Dickens)

bye-spots NOUN bye-spots are lonely places ❑ *and bye-spots of tales rich with indigenous produce* (*The Prelude* by William Wordsworth)

calico NOUN calico is plain white fabric made from cotton ❑ *There was two old dirty calico dresses* (*The Adventures of Huckleberry Finn* by Mark Twain)

camp-fever NOUN camp-fever was another word for the disease typhus ❑ *during a severe camp-fever* (*Emma* by Jane Austen)

cant NOUN cant is insincere or empty talk ❑ *'Man,' said the Ghost, 'if man you be in heart, not adamant, forbear that wicked cant until you have discovered What the surplus is, and Where it is.'* (*A Christmas Carol* by Charles Dickens)

canty ADJ canty means lively, full of life ❑ *My mother lived til eighty, a canty dame to the last* (*Wuthering Heights* by Emily Brontë)

canvas VERB to canvas is to discuss ❑ *We think so very differently on this point Mr Knightley, that there can be no use in canvassing it* (*Emma* by Jane Austen)

capital ADJ capital means excellent or extremely good ❑ *for it's capital, so shady, light, and big* (*Little Women* by Louisa May Alcott)

capstan NOUN a capstan is a device used on a ship to lift sails and anchors ❑ *capstans going, ships going out to sea, and unintelligible sea creatures roaring curses over the* bulwarks at respondent lightermen (*Great Expectations* by Charles Dickens)

case-bottle NOUN a square bottle designed to fit with others into a case ❏ *The spirit being set before him in a huge case-bottle, which had originally come out of some ship's locker* (*The Old Curiosity Shop* by Charles Dickens)

casement NOUN casement is a word meaning window. The teacher in *Nicholas Nickleby* misspells window showing what a bad teacher he is ❏ *W-i-n, win, d-e-r, der, winder, a casement.* (*Nicholas Nickleby* by Charles Dickens)

cataleptic ADJ a cataleptic fit is one in which the victim goes into a trancelike state and remains still for a long time ❏ *It was at this point in their history that Silas's cataleptic fit occurred during the prayer-meeting* (*Silas Marner* by George Eliot)

cauldron NOUN a cauldron is a large cooking pot made of metal ❏ *stirring a large cauldron which seemed to be full of soup* (*Alice's Adventures in Wonderland* by Lewis Carroll)

cephalic ADJ cephalic means to do with the head ❏ *with ink composed of a cephalic tincture* (*Gulliver's Travels* by Jonathan Swift)

chaise and four NOUN a closed four-wheel carriage pulled by four horses ❏ *he came down on Monday in a chaise and four to see the place* (*Pride and Prejudice* by Jane Austen)

chamberlain NOUN the main servant in a household ❏ *In those times a bed was always to be got there at any hour of the night, and the chamberlain, letting me in at his ready wicket, lighted the candle next in order on his shelf* (*Great Expectations* by Charles Dickens)

characters NOUN distinguishing marks ❏ *Impressed upon all forms the characters* (*The Prelude* by William Wordsworth)

chary ADJ cautious ❏ *I should have been chary of discussing my guardian too freely even with her* (*Great Expectations* by Charles Dickens)

cherishes VERB here cherishes means cheers or brightens ❏ *some philosophic song of Truth that cherishes our daily life* (*The Prelude* by William Wordsworth)

chickens' meat PHRASE chickens' meat is an old term which means chickens' feed or food ❏ *I had shook a bag of chickens' meat out in that place* (*Robinson Crusoe* by Daniel Defoe)

chimeras NOUN a chimera is an unrealistic idea or a wish which is unlikely to be fulfilled ❏ *with many other wild impossible chimeras* (*Gulliver's Travels* by Jonathan Swift)

chines NOUN chine is a cut of meat that includes part or all of the backbone of the animal ❏ *and they found hams and chines uncut* (*Silas Marner* by George Eliot)

chits NOUN chits is a slang word which means girls ❏ *I hate affected, niminy-piminy chits!* (*Little Women* by Louisa May Alcott)

chopped VERB chopped means come suddenly or accidentally ❏ *if I had chopped upon them* (*Robinson Crusoe* by Daniel Defoe)

chute NOUN a narrow channel ❏ *One morning about day-break, I found a canoe and crossed over a chute to the main shore* (*The Adventures of Huckleberry Finn* by Mark Twain)

circumspection NOUN careful observation of events and circumstances; caution ❏ *I honour your circumspection* (*Pride and Prejudice* by Jane Austen)

clambered VERB clambered means to climb somewhere with difficulty, usually using your hands and your feet ❏ *he clambered up and down stairs* (*Treasure Island* by Robert Louis Stevenson)

clime NOUN climate ❏ *no season knows nor clime* (*The Sun Rising* by John Donne)

clinched VERB clenched ❏ *the tops whereof I could but just reach with my fist clinched* (*Gulliver's Travels* by Jonathan Swift)

close chair NOUN a close chair is a sedan chair, which is an covered chair which has room for one person. The sedan chair is carried on two poles by two men, one in front and one behind ❏ *persuaded even the Empress herself to let me hold her in her close chair* (*Gulliver's Travels* by Jonathan Swift)

clown NOUN clown here means peasant or person who lives off the land ❏ *In ancient days by emperor and clown* (*Ode on a Nightingale* by John Keats)

coalheaver NOUN a coalheaver loaded coal onto ships using a spade ❏ *Good, strong, wholesome medicine, as was given with great success to two Irish labourers and a coalheaver* (*Oliver Twist* by Charles Dickens)

coal-whippers NOUN men who worked at docks using machines to load coal onto ships ❏ *here, were colliers by the score and score, with the coal-whippers plunging off stages on deck* (*Great Expectations* by Charles Dickens)

cobweb NOUN a cobweb is the net which a spider makes for catching insects ❏ *the walls and ceilings were all hung round with cobwebs* (*Gulliver's Travels* by Jonathan Swift)

coddling VERB coddling means to treat someone too kindly or protect them too much ❏ *and I've been coddling the fellow as if I'd been his grand-mother* (*Little Women* by Louisa May Alcott)

coil NOUN coil means noise or fuss or disturbance ❏ *What a coil is there?* (*Doctor Faustus 4.7* by Christopher Marlowe)

collared VERB to collar something is a slang term which means to capture.

In this sentence, it means he stole it [the money] ❏ *he collared it* (*The Adventures of Huckleberry Finn* by Mark Twain)

colling VERB colling is an old word which means to embrace and kiss ❏ *and no clasping and colling at all* (*Tess of the D'Urbervilles* by Thomas Hardy)

colloquies NOUN colloquy is a formal conversation or dialogue ❏ *Such colloquies have occupied many a pair of pale-faced weavers* (*Silas Marner* by George Eliot)

comfit NOUN sugar-covered pieces of fruit or nut eaten as sweets ❏ *and pulled out a box of comfits* (*Alice's Adventures in Wonderland* by Lewis Carroll)

coming out VERB when a girl came out in society it meant she was of marriageable age. In order to 'come out' girls were expecting to attend balls and other parties during a season ❏ *The younger girls formed hopes of coming out a year or two sooner than they might otherwise have done* (*Pride and Prejudice* by Jane Austen)

commit VERB commit means arrest or stop ❏ *Commit the rascals* (*Doctor Faustus 4.7* by Christopher Marlowe)

commodious ADJ commodious means convenient ❏ *the most commodious and effectual ways* (*Gulliver's Travels* by Jonathan Swift)

commons NOUN commons is an old term meaning food shared with others ❏ *his pauper assistants ranged themselves behind him; the gruel was served out; and a long grace was said over the short commons.* (*Oliver Twist* by Charles Dickens)

complacency NOUN here complacency means a desire to please others. To-day complacency means feeling pleased with oneself without good reason. ❏ *Twas thy power that raised the first complacency in me* (*The Prelude* by William Wordsworth)

complaisance NOUN complaisance was eagerness to please ❑ *we cannot wonder at his complaisance* (*Pride and Prejudice* by Jane Austen)

complaisant ADJ complaisant means polite ❑ *extremely cheerful and complaisant to their guest* (*Gulliver's Travels* by Jonathan Swift)

conning VERB conning means learning by heart ❑ *Or conning more* (*The Prelude* by William Wordsworth)

consequent NOUN consequence ❑ *as avarice is the necessary consequent of old age* (*Gulliver's Travels* by Jonathan Swift)

consorts NOUN concerts ❑ *The King, who delighted in music, had frequent consorts at Court* (*Gulliver's Travels* by Jonathan Swift)

conversible ADJ conversible meant easy to talk to, companionable ❑ *He can be a conversible companion* (*Pride and Prejudice* by Jane Austen)

copper NOUN a copper is a large pot that can be heated directly over a fire ❑ *He gazed in stupefied astonishment on the small rebel for some seconds, and then clung for support to the copper* (*Oliver Twist* by Charles Dickens)

copper-stick NOUN a copper-stick is the long piece of wood used to stir washing in the copper (or boiler) which was usually the biggest cooking pot in the house ❑ *It was Christmas Eve, and I had to stir the pudding for next day, with a copper-stick, from seven to eight by the Dutch clock* (*Great Expectations* by Charles Dickens)

counting-house NOUN a counting-house is a place where accountants work ❑ *Once upon a time–of all the good days in the year, on Christmas Eve–old Scrooge sat busy in his counting-house* (*A Christmas Carol* by Charles Dickens)

courtier NOUN a courtier is someone who attends the king or queen–a member of the court ❑ *next the ten courtiers;* (*Alice's Adventures in Wonderland* by Lewis Carroll)

covies NOUN covies were flocks of partridges ❑ *and will save all of the best covies for you* (*Pride and Prejudice* by Jane Austen)

cowed VERB cowed means frightened or intimidated ❑ *it cowed me more than the pain* (*Treasure Island* by Robert Louis Stevenson)

cozened VERB cozened means tricked or deceived ❑ *Do you remember, sir, how you cozened me* (*Doctor Faustus 4.7* by Christopher Marlowe)

cravats NOUN a cravat is a folded cloth that a man wears wrapped around his neck as a decorative item of clothing ❑ *we'd 'a' slept in our cravats to-night* (*The Adventures of Huckleberry Finn* by Mark Twain)

crock and dirt PHRASE crock and dirt is an old expression meaning soot and dirt ❑ *and the mare catching cold at the door, and the boy grimed with crock and dirt* (*Great Expectations* by Charles Dickens)

crockery NOUN here crockery means pottery ❑ *By one of the parrots was a cat made of crockery* (*The Adventures of Huckleberry Finn* by Mark Twain)

crooked sixpence PHRASE it was considered unlucky to have a bent sixpence ❑ *You've got the beauty, you see, and I've got the luck, so you must keep me by you for your crooked sixpence* (*Silas Marner* by George Eliot)

croquet NOUN croquet is a traditional English summer game in which players try to hit wooden balls through hoops ❑ *and once she remembered trying to box her own ears for having cheated herself in a game of croquet* (*Alice's Adventures in Wonderland* by Lewis Carroll)

cross PREP across ❑ *The two great streets, which run cross and divide it into four quarters* (*Gulliver's Travels* by Jonathan Swift)

culpable ADJ if you are culpable for something it means you are to blame ❏ *deep are the sorrows that spring from false ideas for which no man is culpable.* (*Silas Marner* by George Eliot)

cultured ADJ cultivated ❏ *Nor less when spring had warmed the cultured Vale* (*The Prelude* by William Wordsworth)

cupidity NOUN cupidity is greed ❏ *These people hated me with the hatred of cupidity and disappoint-ment.* (*Great Expectations* by Charles Dickens)

curricle NOUN an open two-wheeled carriage with one seat for the driver and space for a single passenger ❏ *and they saw a lady and a gentleman in a curricle* (*Pride and Prejudice* by Jane Austen)

cynosure NOUN a cynosure is something that strongly attracts attention or admiration ❏ *Then I thought of Eliza and Georgiana; I beheld one the cynosure of a ballroom, the other the inmate of a convent cell* (*Jane Eyre* by Charlotte Brontë)

dalliance NOUN someone's dalliance with something is a brief involve-ment with it ❏ *nor sporting in the dalliance of love* (*Doctor Faustus Chorus* by Christopher Marlowe)

darkling ADV darkling is an archaic way of saying in the dark ❏ *Darkling I listen* (*Ode on a Nightingale* by John Keats)

delf-case NOUN a sideboard for holding dishes and crockery ❏ *at the pewter dishes and delf-case* (*Wuthering Heights* by Emily Brontë)

determined ■ VERB here determined means ended ❏ *and be out of vogue when that was determined* (*Gulliver's Travels* by Jonathan Swift) ■ VERB determined can mean to have been learned or found espe-cially by investigation or experience ❏ *All the sensitive feelings it wounded so cruelly, all the shame and misery it kept alive within my breast, became more poignant as I*

thought of this; and I determined that the life was unendurable (*David Copperfield* by Charles Dickens)

Deuce NOUN a slang term for the Devil ❏ *Ah, I dare say I did. Deuce take me, he added suddenly, I know I did. I find I am not quite unscrewed yet.* (*Great Expectations* by Charles Dickens)

diabolical ADJ diabolical means devilish or evil ❏ *and with a thou-sand diabolical expressions* (*Treasure Island* by Robert Louis Stevenson)

direction NOUN here direction means address ❏ *Elizabeth was not surprised at it, as Jane had written the direction remarkably ill* (*Pride and Prejudice* by Jane Austen)

discover VERB to make known or announce ❏ *the Emperor would discover the secret while I was out of his power* (*Gulliver's Travels* by Jonathan Swift)

dissemble VERB hide or conceal ❏ *Dissemble nothing* (*On His Mistress* by John Donne)

dissolve VERB dissolve here means to release from life, to die ❏ *Fade far away, dissolve, and quite forget* (*Ode on a Nightingale* by John Keats)

distrain VERB to distrain is to seize the property of someone who is in debt in compensation for the money owed ❏ *for he's threatening to distrain for it* (*Silas Marner* by George Eliot)

Divan NOUN a Divan was originally a Turkish council of state–the name was transferred to the couches they sat on and is used to mean this in English ❏ *Mr Brass applauded this picture very much, and the bed being soft and comfortable, Mr Quilp determined to use it, both as a sleeping place by night and as a kind of Divan by day.* (*The Old Curiosity Shop* by Charles Dickens)

divorcement NOUN separation ❏ *By all pains which want and divorcement* *hath* (*On His Mistress* by John Donne)

dog in the manger, PHRASE this phrase describes someone who prevents you from enjoying something that they themselves have no need for ❑ *You are a dog in the manger, Cathy, and desire no one to be loved but yourself* (*Wuthering Heights* by Emily Brontë)

dolorifuge NOUN dolorifuge is a word which Thomas Hardy invented. It means pain-killer or comfort ❑ *as a species of dolorifuge* (*Tess of the D'Urbervilles* by Thomas Hardy)

dome NOUN building ❑ *that river and that mouldering dome* (*The Prelude* by William Wordsworth)

domestic NOUN here domestic means a person's management of the house ❑ *to give some account of my domestic* (*Gulliver's Travels* by Jonathan Swift)

dunce NOUN a dunce is another word for idiot ❑ *Do you take me for a dunce? Go on?* (*Alice's Adventures in Wonderland* by Lewis Carroll)

Ecod EXCLAM a slang exclamation meaning 'oh God!' ❑ *'Ecod,' replied Wemmick, shaking his head, 'that's not my trade.'* (*Great Expectations* by Charles Dickens)

egg-hot NOUN an egg-hot (see also 'flip' and 'negus') was a hot drink made from beer and eggs, sweetened with nutmeg ❑ *She fainted when she saw me return, and made a little jug of egg-hot afterwards to console us while we talked it over.* (*David Copperfield* by Charles Dickens)

encores NOUN an encore is a short extra performance at the end of a longer one, which the entertainer gives because the audience has enthusiastically asked for it ❑ *we want a little something to answer encores with, anyway* (*The Adventures of Huckleberry Finn* by Mark Twain)

equipage NOUN an elegant and impressive carriage ❑ *and besides, the equipage did not answer to any of*

their neighbours (*Pride and Prejudice* by Jane Austen)

exordium NOUN an exordium is the opening part of a speech ❑ *'Now, Handel,' as if it were the grave beginning of a portentous business exordium, he had suddenly given up that tone* (*Great Expectations* by Charles Dickens)

expect VERB here expect means to wait for ❑ *to expect his farther commands* (*Gulliver's Travels* by Jonathan Swift)

familiars NOUN familiars means spirits or devils who come to someone when they are called ❑ *I'll turn all the lice about thee into familiars* (*Doctor Faustus 1.4* by Christopher Marlowe)

fantods NOUN a fantod is a person who fidgets or can't stop moving nervously ❑ *It most give me the fantods* (*The Adventures of Huckleberry Finn* by Mark Twain)

farthing NOUN a farthing is an old unit of British currency which was worth a quarter of a penny ❑ *Not a farthing less. A great many back-payments are included in it, I assure you.* (*A Christmas Carol* by Charles Dickens)

farthingale NOUN a hoop worn under a skirt to extend it ❑ *A bell with an old voice–which I dare say in its time had often said to the house, Here is the green farthingale* (*Great Expectations* by Charles Dickens)

favours NOUN here favours is an old word which means ribbons ❑ *A group of humble mourners entered the gate: wearing white favours* (*Oliver Twist* by Charles Dickens)

feigned VERB pretend or pretending ❑ *not my feigned page* (*On His Mistress* by John Donne)

fence ■ NOUN a fence is someone who receives and sells stolen goods ❑ *What are you up to? Ill-treating the boys, you covetous, avaricious, in-sa-ti-a-ble old fence?* (*Oliver Twist* by

Charles Dickens) ■ NOUN defence or protection ❏ *but honesty hath no fence against superior cunning* (Gulliver's Travels by Jonathan Swift)

fess ADJ fess is an old word which means pleased or proud ❏ *You'll be fess enough, my poppet* (Tess of the D'Urbervilles by Thomas Hardy)

fettered ADJ fettered means bound in chains or chained ❏ *'You are fettered,' said Scrooge, trembling. 'Tell me why?'* (A Christmas Carol by Charles Dickens)

fidges VERB fidges means fidgets, which is to keep moving your hands slightly because you are nervous or excited ❏ *Look, Jim, how my fingers fidges* (Treasure Island by Robert Louis Stevenson)

finger-post NOUN a finger-post is a sign-post showing the direction to different places ❏ *'The gallows,' continued Fagin, 'the gallows, my dear, is an ugly finger-post, which points out a very short and sharp turning that has stopped many a bold fellow's career on the broad highway.'* (Oliver Twist by Charles Dickens)

fire-irons NOUN fire-irons are tools kept by the side of the fire to either cook with or look after the fire ❏ *the fire-irons came first* (Alice's Adventures in Wonderland by Lewis Carroll)

fire-plug NOUN a fire-plug is another word for a fire hydrant ❏ *The pony looked with great attention into a fire-plug, which was near him, and appeared to be quite absorbed in contemplating it* (The Old Curiosity Shop by Charles Dickens)

flank NOUN flank is the side of an animal ❏ *And all her silken flanks with garlands dressed* (Ode on a Grecian Urn by John Keats)

flip NOUN a flip is a drink made from warmed ale, sugar, spice and beaten egg ❏ *The events of the day, in combination with the twins, if not with the flip, had made Mrs.*

Micawber hysterical, and she shed tears as she replied (David Copperfield by Charles Dickens)

flit VERB flit means to move quickly ❏ *and if he had meant to flit to Thrushcross Grange* (Wuthering Heights by Emily Brontë)

floorcloth NOUN a floorcloth was a hard-wearing piece of canvas used instead of carpet ❏ *This avenging phantom was ordered to be on duty at eight on Tuesday morning in the hall (it was two feet square, as charged for floorcloth)* (Great Expectations by Charles Dickens)

fly-driver NOUN a fly-driver is a carriage drawn by a single horse ❏ *The fly-drivers, among whom I inquired next, were equally jocose and equally disrespectful* (David Copperfield by Charles Dickens)

fob NOUN a small pocket in which a watch is kept ❏ *'Certain,' replied the man, drawing a gold watch from his fob* (Oliver Twist by Charles Dickens)

folly NOUN folly means foolishness or stupidity ❏ *the folly of beginning a work* (Robinson Crusoe by Daniel Defoe)

fond ADJ fond means foolish ❏ *Fond worldling* (Doctor Faustus 5.2 by Christopher Marlowe)

fondness NOUN silly or foolish affection ❏ *They have no fondness for their colts or foals* (Gulliver's Travels by Jonathan Swift)

for his fancy PHRASE for his fancy means for his liking or as he wanted ❏ *and as I did not obey quick enough for his fancy* (Treasure Island by Robert Louis Stevenson)

forlorn ADJ lost or very upset ❏ *you are from that day forlorn* (Gulliver's Travels by Jonathan Swift)

foster-sister NOUN a foster-sister was someone brought up by the same nurse or in the same household ❏ *I had been his foster-sister* (Wuthering Heights by Emily Brontë)

fox-fire NOUN fox-fire is a weak glow that is given off by decaying, rotten wood ❑ *what we must have was a lot of them rotten chunks that's called fox-fire* (*The Adventures of Huckleberry Finn* by Mark Twain)

frozen sea PHRASE the Arctic Ocean ❑ *into the frozen sea* (*Gulliver's Travels* by Jonathan Swift)

gainsay VERB to gainsay something is to say it isn't true or to deny it ❑ *'So she had,' cried Scrooge. 'You're right. I'll not gainsay it, Spirit. God forbid!'* (*A Christmas Carol* by Charles Dickens)

gaiters NOUN gaiters were leggings made of a cloth or piece of leather which covered the leg from the knee to the ankle ❑ *Mr Knightley was hard at work upon the lower buttons of his thick leather gaiters* (*Emma* by Jane Austen)

galluses NOUN galluses is an old spelling of gallows, and here means suspenders. Suspenders are straps worn over someone's shoulders and fastened to their trousers to prevent the trousers falling down ❑ *and home-knit galluses* (*The Adventures of Huckleberry Finn* by Mark Twain)

galoot NOUN a sailor but also a clumsy person ❑ *and maybe a galoot on it chopping* (*The Adventures of Huckleberry Finn* by Mark Twain)

gayest ADJ gayest means the most lively and bright or merry ❑ *Beth played her gayest march* (*Little Women* by Louisa May Alcott)

gem NOUN here gem means jewellery ❑ *the mountain shook off turf and flower, had only heath for raiment and crag for gem* (*Jane Eyre* by Charlotte Brontë)

giddy ADJ giddy means dizzy ❑ *and I wish you wouldn't keep appearing and vanishing so suddenly; you make one quite giddy.* (*Alice's Adventures in Wonderland* by Lewis Carroll)

gig NOUN a light two-wheeled carriage ❑ *when a gig drove up to the garden gate: out of which there jumped a fat gentleman* (*Oliver Twist* by Charles Dickens)

gladsome ADJ gladsome is an old word meaning glad or happy ❑ *Nobody ever stopped him in the street to say, with gladsome looks* (*A Christmas Carol* by Charles Dickens)

glen NOUN a glen is a small valley; the word is used commonly in Scotland ❑ *a beck which follows the bend of the glen* (*Wuthering Heights* by Emily Brontë)

gravelled VERB gravelled is an old term which means to baffle or defeat someone ❑ *Gravelled the pastors of the German Church* (*Doctor Faustus 1.1* by Christopher Marlowe)

grinder NOUN a grinder was a private tutor ❑ *but that when he had had the happiness of marrying Mrs Pocket very early in his life, he had impaired his prospects and taken up the calling of a Grinder* (*Great Expectations* by Charles Dickens)

gruel NOUN gruel is a thin, watery cornmeal or oatmeal soup ❑ *and the little saucepan of gruel (Scrooge had a cold in his head) upon the hob.* (*A Christmas Carol* by Charles Dickens)

guinea, half a NOUN half a guinea was ten shillings and sixpence ❑ *but lay out half a guinea at Ford's* (*Emma* by Jane Austen)

gull VERB gull is an old term which means to fool or deceive someone ❑ *Hush, I'll gull him supernaturally* (*Doctor Faustus 3.4* by Christopher Marlowe)

gunnel NOUN the gunnel, or gunwale, is the upper edge of a boat's side ❑ *But he put his foot on the gunnel and rocked her* (*The Adventures of Huckleberry Finn* by Mark Twain)

gunwale NOUN the side of a ship ❑ *He dipped his hand in the water over the boat's gunwale* (*Great Expectations* by Charles Dickens)

Gytrash NOUN a Gytrash is an omen of misfortune to the superstitious, usually taking the form of a hound ❑ *I remembered certain of Bessie's tales, wherein figured a North-of-England spirit, called a 'Gytrash'* (*Jane Eyre* by Charlotte Brontë)

hackney-cabriolet NOUN a two-wheeled carriage with four seats for hire and pulled by a horse ❑ *A hackney-cabriolet was in waiting; with the same vehemence which she had exhibited in addressing Oliver, the girl pulled him in with her, and drew the curtains close.* (*Oliver Twist* by Charles Dickens)

hackney-coach NOUN a four-wheeled horse-drawn vehicle for hire ❑ *The twilight was beginning to close in, when Mr. Brownlow alighted from a hackney-coach at his own door, and knocked softly.* (*Oliver Twist* by Charles Dickens)

haggler NOUN a haggler is someone who travels from place to place selling small goods and items ❑ *when I be plain Jack Durbeyfield, the haggler* (*Tess of the D'Urbervilles* by Thomas Hardy)

halter NOUN a halter is a rope or strap used to lead an animal or to tie it up ❑ *I had of course long been used to a halter and a headstall* (*Black Beauty* by Anna Sewell)

hamlet NOUN a hamlet is a small village or a group of houses in the countryside ❑ *down from the hamlet* (*Treasure Island* by Robert Louis Stevenson)

hand-barrow NOUN a hand-barrow is a device for carrying heavy objects. It is like a wheelbarrow except that it has handles, rather than wheels, for moving the barrow ❑ *his sea chest following behind him in a hand-barrow* (*Treasure Island* by Robert Louis Stevenson)

handspike NOUN a handspike was a stick which was used as a lever ❑ *a bit of stick like a handspike* (*Treasure Island* by Robert Louis Stevenson)

haply ADV haply means by chance or perhaps ❑ *And haply the Queen-Moon is on her throne* (*Ode on a Nightingale* by John Keats)

harem NOUN the harem was the part of the house where the women lived ❑ *mostly they hang round the harem* (*The Adventures of Huckleberry Finn* by Mark Twain)

hautboys NOUN hautboys are oboes ❑ *sausages and puddings resembling flutes and hautboys* (*Gulliver's Travels* by Jonathan Swift)

hawker NOUN a hawker is someone who sells goods to people as he travels rather than from a fixed place like a shop ❑ *to buy some stockings from a hawker* (*Treasure Island* by Robert Louis Stevenson)

hawser NOUN a hawser is a rope used to tie up or tow a ship or boat ❑ *Again among the tiers of shipping, in and out, avoiding rusty chain-cables, frayed hempen hawsers* (*Great Expectations* by Charles Dickens)

headstall NOUN the headstall is the part of the bridle or halter that goes around a horse's head ❑ *I had of course long been used to a halter and a headstall* (*Black Beauty* by Anna Sewell)

hearken VERB hearken means to listen ❑ *though we sometimes stopped to lay hold of each other and hearken* (*Treasure Island* by Robert Louis Stevenson)

heartless ADJ here heartless means without heart or dejected ❑ *I am not heartless* (*The Prelude* by William Wordsworth)

hebdomadal ADJ hebdomadal means weekly ❑ *It was the hebdomadal treat to which we all looked forward from Sabbath to Sabbath* (*Jane Eyre* by Charlotte Brontë)

highwaymen NOUN highwaymen were people who stopped travellers and robbed them ❑ *We are high-waymen* (*The Adventures of Huckleberry Finn* by Mark Twain)

hinds NOUN hinds means farm hands, or people who work on a farm ❑ *He called his hinds about him* (*Gulliver's Travels* by Jonathan Swift)

histrionic ADJ if you refer to someone's behaviour as histrionic, you are being critical of it because it is dramatic and exaggerated ❑ *But the histrionic muse is the darling* (*The Adventures of Huckleberry Finn* by Mark Twain)

hogs NOUN hogs is another word for pigs ❑ *Tom called the hogs 'ingots'* (*The Adventures of Huckleberry Finn* by Mark Twain)

horrors NOUN the horrors are a fit, called delirium tremens, which is caused by drinking too much alcohol ❑ *I'll have the horrors* (*Treasure Island* by Robert Louis Stevenson)

huffy ADJ huffy means to be obviously annoyed or offended about something ❑ *They will feel that more than angry speeches or huffy actions* (*Little Women* by Louisa May Alcott)

hulks NOUN hulks were prison-ships ❑ *The miserable companion of thieves and ruffians, the fallen outcast of low haunts, the associate of the scourings of the jails and hulks* (*Oliver Twist* by Charles Dickens)

humbug NOUN humbug means nonsense or rubbish ❑ *'Bah,' said Scrooge. 'Humbug!'* (*A Christmas Carol* by Charles Dickens)

humours NOUN it was believed that there were four fluids in the body called humours which decided the temperament of a person depending on how much of each fluid was present ❑ *other peccant humours* (*Gulliver's Travels* by Jonathan Swift)

husbandry NOUN husbandry is farming animals ❑ *bad husbandry were plentifully anointing their wheels* (*Silas Marner* by George Eliot)

huswife NOUN a huswife was a small sewing kit ❑ *but I had put my huswife on it* (*Emma* by Jane Austen)

ideal ADJ ideal in this context means imaginary ❑ *I discovered the yell was not ideal* (*Wuthering Heights* by Emily Brontë)

If our two PHRASE if both our ❑ *If our two loves be one* (*The Good-Morrow* by John Donne)

ignis-fatuus NOUN ignis-fatuus is the light given out by burning marsh gases, which lead careless travellers into danger ❑ *it is madness in all women to let a secret love kindle within them, which, if unreturned and unknown, must devour the life that feeds it; and, if discovered and responded to, must lead ignis-fatuus-like, into miry wilds whence there is no extrication.* (*Jane Eyre* by Charlotte Brontë)

imaginations NOUN here imaginations means schemes or plans ❑ *soon drove out those imaginations* (*Gulliver's Travels* by Jonathan Swift)

impressible ADJ impressible means open or impressionable ❑ *for Marner had one of those impressible, self-doubting natures* (*Silas Marner* by George Eliot)

in good intelligence PHRASE friendly with each other ❑ *that these two persons were in good intelligence with each other* (*Gulliver's Travels* by Jonathan Swift)

inanity NOUN inanity is silliness or dull stupidity ❑ *Do we not wile away moments of inanity* (*Silas Marner* by George Eliot)

incivility NOUN incivility means rudeness or impoliteness ❑ *if it's only for a piece of incivility like to-night's* (*Treasure Island* by Robert Louis Stevenson)

indigenae NOUN indigenae means natives or people from that area ❑ *an exotic that the surly indigenae will not recognise for kin* (*Wuthering Heights* by Emily Brontë)

indocible ADJ unteachable ❑ *so they were the most restive and indocible* (*Gulliver's Travels* by Jonathan Swift)

ingenuity NOUN inventiveness ❑ *entreated me to give him something as an encouragement to ingenuity* (*Gulliver's Travels* by Jonathan Swift)

ingots NOUN an ingot is a lump of a valuable metal like gold, usually shaped like a brick ❑ *Tom called the hogs 'ingots'* (*The Adventures of Huckleberry Finn* by Mark Twain)

inkstand NOUN an inkstand is a pot which was put on a desk to contain either ink or pencils and pens ❑ *throwing an inkstand at the Lizard as she spoke* (*Alice's Adventures in Wonderland* by Lewis Carroll)

inordinate ADJ without order. To-day inordinate means 'excessive'. ❑ *Though yet untutored and inordinate* (*The Prelude* by William Wordsworth)

intellectuals NOUN here intellectuals means the minds (of the workmen) ❑ *those instructions they give being too refined for the intellectuals of their workmen* (*Gulliver's Travels* by Jonathan Swift)

interview NOUN meeting ❑ *By our first strange and fatal interview* (*On His Mistress* by John Donne)

jacks NOUN jacks are rods for turning a spit over a fire ❑ *It was a small bit of pork suspended from the kettle hanger by a string passed through a large door key, in a way known to primitive housekeepers unpossessed of jacks* (*Silas Marner* by George Eliot)

jews-harp NOUN a jews-harp is a small, metal, musical instrument that is played by the mouth ❑ *A jews-harp's plenty good enough for a rat* (*The Adventures of Huckleberry Finn* by Mark Twain)

jorum NOUN a large bowl ❑ *while Miss Skiffins brewed such a jorum of tea, that the pig in the back premises became strongly excited* (*Great Expectations* by Charles Dickens)

jostled VERB jostled means bumped or pushed by someone or some people

❑ *being jostled himself into the kennel* (*Gulliver's Travels* by Jonathan Swift)

keepsake NOUN a keepsake is a gift which reminds someone of an event or of the person who gave it to them. ❑ *books and ornaments they had in their boudoirs at home: keepsakes that different relations had presented to them* (*Jane Eyre* by Charlotte Brontë)

kenned VERB kenned means knew ❑ *though little kenned the lamplighter that he had any company but Christmas!* (*A Christmas Carol* by Charles Dickens)

kennel NOUN kennel means gutter, which is the edge of a road next to the pavement, where rain water collects and flows away ❑ *being jostled himself into the kennel* (*Gulliver's Travels* by Jonathan Swift)

knock-knee ADJ knock-knee means slanted, at an angle. ❑ *LOT 1 was marked in whitewashed knock-knee letters on the brewhouse* (*Great Expectations* by Charles Dickens)

ladylike ADJ to be ladylike is to behave in a polite, dignified and graceful way ❑ *No, winking isn't ladylike* (*Little Women* by Louisa May Alcott)

lapse NOUN flow ❑ *Stealing with silent lapse to join the brook* (*The Prelude* by William Wordsworth)

larry NOUN larry is an old word which means commotion or noisy celebration ❑ *That was all a part of the larry!* (*Tess of the D'Urbervilles* by Thomas Hardy)

laths NOUN laths are strips of wood ❑ *The panels shrunk, the windows cracked; fragments of plaster fell out of the ceiling, and the naked laths were shown instead* (*A Christmas Carol* by Charles Dickens)

leer NOUN a leer is an unpleasant smile ❑ *with a kind of leer* (*Treasure Island* by Robert Louis Stevenson)

lenitives NOUN these are different kinds of drugs or medicines: lenitives and palliatives were pain relievers; aperitives were laxatives; abstersives caused vomiting; corrosives destroyed human tissue; restringents caused constipation; cephalalgics stopped headaches; icterics were used as medicine for jaundice; apophlegmatics were cough medicine, and acoustics were cures for the loss of hearing ❑ *lenitives, aperitives, abstersives, corrosives, restringents, palliatives, laxatives, cephalalgics, icterics, apophlegmatics, acoustics* (*Gulliver's Travels* by Jonathan Swift)

lest CONJ in case. If you do something lest something (usually) unpleasant happens you do it to try to prevent it happening ❑ *She went in without knocking, and hurried upstairs, in great fear lest she should meet the real Mary Ann* (*Alice's Adventures in Wonderland* by Lewis Carroll)

levee NOUN a levee is an old term for a meeting held in the morning, shortly after the person holding the meeting has got out of bed ❑ *I used to attend the King's levee once or twice a week* (*Gulliver's Travels* by Jonathan Swift)

life-preserver NOUN a club which had lead inside it to make it heavier and therefore more dangerous ❑ *and with no more suspicious articles displayed to view than two or three heavy bludgeons which stood in a corner, and a 'life-preserver' that hung over the chimney-piece.* (*Oliver Twist* by Charles Dickens)

lighterman NOUN a lighterman is another word for sailor ❑ *in and out, hammers going in ship-builders' yards, saws going at timber, clashing engines going at things unknown, pumps going in leaky ships, capstans going, ships going out to sea, and unintelligible sea creatures roaring curses over the bulwarks at respondent lightermen* (*Great Expectations* by Charles Dickens)

livery NOUN servants often wore a uniform known as a livery ❑ *suddenly a footman in livery came running out of the wood* (*Alice's Adventures in Wonderland* by Lewis Carroll)

livid ADJ livid means pale or ash coloured. Livid also means very angry ❑ *a dirty, livid white* (*Treasure Island* by Robert Louis Stevenson)

lottery-tickets NOUN a popular card game ❑ *and Mrs. Philips protested that they would have a nice comfortable noisy game of lottery tickets* (*Pride and Prejudice* by Jane Austen)

lower and upper world PHRASE the earth and the heavens are the lower and upper worlds ❑ *the changes in the lower and upper world* (*Gulliver's Travels* by Jonathan Swift)

lustres NOUN lustres are chandeliers. A chandelier is a large, decorative frame which holds light bulbs or candles and hangs from the ceiling ❑ *the lustres, lights, the carving and the guilding* (*The Prelude* by William Wordsworth)

lynched VERB killed without a criminal trial by a crowd of people ❑ *He'll never know how nigh he come to getting lynched* (*The Adventures of Huckleberry Finn* by Mark Twain)

malingering VERB if someone is malingering they are pretending to be ill to avoid working ❑ *And you stand there malingering* (*Treasure Island* by Robert Louis Stevenson)

managing PHRASE treating with consideration ❑ *to think the honour of my own kind not worth managing* (*Gulliver's Travels* by Jonathan Swift)

manhood PHRASE manhood means human nature ❑ *concerning the nature of manhood* (*Gulliver's Travels* by Jonathan Swift)

man-trap NOUN a man-trap is a set of steel jaws that snap shut when trodden on and trap a person's leg

❑ *'Don't go to him,' I called out of the window, 'he's an assassin! A man-trap!'* (*Oliver Twist* by Charles Dickens)

maps NOUN charts of the night sky ❑ *Let maps to others, worlds on worlds have shown* (*The Good-Morrow* by John Donne)

mark VERB look at or notice ❑ *Mark but this flea, and mark in this* (*The Flea* by John Donne)

maroons NOUN A maroon is someone who has been left in a place which it is difficult for them to escape from, like a small island ❑ *if schooners, islands, and maroons* (*Treasure Island* by Robert Louis Stevenson)

mast NOUN here mast means the fruit of forest trees ❑ *a quantity of acorns, dates, chestnuts, and other mast* (*Gulliver's Travels* by Jonathan Swift)

mate VERB defeat ❑ *Where Mars did mate the warlike Carthigens* (*Doctor Faustus Chorus* by Christopher Marlowe)

mealy ADJ Mealy when used to describe a face meant pallid, pale or colourless ❑ *I only know two sorts of boys. Mealy boys, and beef-faced boys* (*Oliver Twist* by Charles Dickens)

middling ADV fairly or moderately ❑ *she worked me middling hard for about an hour* (*The Adventures of Huckleberry Finn* by Mark Twain)

mill NOUN a mill, or treadmill, was a device for hard labour or punishment in prison ❑ *Was you never on the mill?* (*Oliver Twist* by Charles Dickens)

milliner's shop NOUN a milliner's sold fabrics, clothing, lace and accessories; as time went on they specialized more and more in hats ❑ *to pay their duty to their aunt and to a milliner's shop just over the way* (*Pride and Prejudice* by Jane Austen)

minching un' munching PHRASE how people in the north of England used to describe the way people

from the south speak ❑ *Minching un' munching!* (*Wuthering Heights* by Emily Brontë)

mine NOUN gold ❑ *Whether both th'Indias of spice and mine* (*The Sun Rising* by John Donne)

mire NOUN mud ❑ *Tis my fate to be always ground into the mire under the iron heel of oppression* (*The Adventures of Huckleberry Finn* by Mark Twain)

miscellany NOUN a miscellany is a collection of many different kinds of things ❑ *under that, the miscellany began* (*Treasure Island* by Robert Louis Stevenson)

mistarshers NOUN mistarshers means moustache, which is the hair that grows on a man's upper lip ❑ *when he put his hand up to his mistarshers* (*Tess of the D'Urbervilles* by Thomas Hardy)

morrow NOUN here good-morrow means tomorrow and a new and better life ❑ *And now good-morrow to our waking souls* (*The Good-Morrow* by John Donne)

mortification NOUN mortification is an old word for gangrene which is when part of the body decays or 'dies' because of disease ❑ *Yes, it was a mortification—that was it* (*The Adventures of Huckleberry Finn* by Mark Twain)

mought VERB mought is an old spelling of might ❑ *what you mought call me? You mought call me captain* (*Treasure Island* by Robert Louis Stevenson)

move VERB move me not means do not make me angry ❑ *Move me not, Faustus* (*Doctor Faustus 2.1* by Christopher Marlowe)

muffin-cap NOUN a muffin-cap is a flat cap made from wool ❑ *the old one, remained stationary in the muffin-cap and leathers* (*Oliver Twist* by Charles Dickens)

mulatter NOUN a mulatter was another word for mulatto, which is a person with parents who are from different races ❏ *a mulatter, most as white as a white man* (*The Adventures of Huckleberry Finn* by Mark Twain)

mummery NOUN mummery is an old word that meant meaningless (or pretentious) ceremony ❏ *When they were all gone, and when Trabb and his men–but not his boy: I looked for him–had crammed their mummery into bags, and were gone too, the house felt wholesomer.* (*Great Expectations* by Charles Dickens)

nap NOUN the nap is the woolly surface on a new item of clothing. Here the surface has been worn away so it looks bare ❏ *like an old hat with the nap rubbed off* (*The Adventures of Huckleberry Finn* by Mark Twain)

natural ◼ NOUN a natural is a person born with learning difficulties ❏ *though he had been left to his particular care by their deceased father, who thought him almost a natural.* (*David Copperfield* by Charles Dickens) ◼ ADJ natural meant illegitimate ❏ *Harriet Smith was the natural daughter of somebody* (*Emma* by Jane Austen)

navigator NOUN a navigator was originally someone employed to dig canals. It is the origin of the word 'navvy' meaning a labourer ❏ *She ascertained from me in a few words what it was all about, comforted Dora, and gradually convinced her that I was not a labourer–from my manner of stating the case I believe Dora concluded that I was a navigator, and went balancing myself up and down a plank all day with a wheelbarrow–and so brought us together in peace.* (*David Copperfield* by Charles Dickens)

necromancy NOUN necromancy means a kind of magic where the magician speaks to spirits or ghosts to find out what will happen in the future ❏ *He surfeits upon cursed necromancy* (*Doctor Faustus chorus* by Christopher Marlowe)

negus NOUN a negus is a hot drink made from sweetened wine and water ❏ *He sat placidly perusing the newspaper, with his little head on one side, and a glass of warm sherry negus at his elbow.* (*David Copperfield* by Charles Dickens)

nice ADJ discriminating. Able to make good judgements or choices ❏ *consequently a claim to be nice* (*Emma* by Jane Austen)

nigh ADV nigh means near ❏ *He'll never know how nigh he come to getting lynched* (*The Adventures of Huckleberry Finn* by Mark Twain)

nimbleness NOUN nimbleness means being able to move very quickly or skilfully ❏ *and with incredible accuracy and nimbleness* (*Treasure Island* by Robert Louis Stevenson)

noggin NOUN a noggin is a small mug or a wooden cup ❏ *you'll bring me one noggin of rum* (*Treasure Island* by Robert Louis Stevenson)

none ADJ neither ❏ *none can die* (*The Good-Morrow* by John Donne)

notices NOUN observations ❏ *Arch are his notices* (*The Prelude* by William Wordsworth)

occiput NOUN occiput means the back of the head ❏ *saw off the occiput of each couple* (*Gulliver's Travels* by Jonathan Swift)

officiously ADV kindly ❏ *the governess who attended Glumdalclitch very officiously lifted me up* (*Gulliver's Travels* by Jonathan Swift)

old salt PHRASE old salt is a slang term for an experienced sailor ❏ *a 'true sea-dog', and a 'real old salt'* (*Treasure Island* by Robert Louis Stevenson)

or ere PHRASE before ❏ *or ere the Hall was built* (*The Prelude* by William Wordsworth)

ostler NOUN one who looks after horses at an inn ❏ *The bill paid, and the waiter remembered, and the ostler not forgotten, and the chambermaid taken into consideration* (*Great Expectations* by Charles Dickens)

ostry NOUN an ostry is an old word for a pub or hotel ❏ *lest I send you into the ostry with a vengeance* (*Doctor Faustus 2.2* by Christopher Marlowe)

outrunning the constable PHRASE outrunning the constable meant spending more than you earn ❏ *but I shall by this means be able to check your bills and to pull you up if I find you outrunning the constable.* (*Great Expectations* by Charles Dickens)

over ADV across ❏ *It is in length six yards, and in the thickest part at least three yards over* (*Gulliver's Travels* by Jonathan Swift)

over the broomstick PHRASE this is a phrase meaning 'getting married without a formal ceremony' ❏ *They both led tramping lives, and this woman in Gerrard-street here, had been married very young, over the broomstick (as we say), to a tramping man, and was a perfect fury in point of jealousy.* (*Great Expectations* by Charles Dickens)

own VERB own means to admit or to acknowledge ❏ *It's my old girl that advises. She has the head. But I never own to it before her. Discipline must be maintained* (*Bleak House* by Charles Dickens)

page NOUN here page means a boy employed to run errands ❏ *not my feigned page* (*On His Mistress* by John Donne)

paid pretty dear PHRASE paid pretty dear means paid a high price or suffered quite a lot ❏ *I paid pretty dear for my monthly fourpenny piece* (*Treasure Island* by Robert Louis Stevenson)

pannikins NOUN pannikins were small tin cups ❏ *of lifting light glasses and cups to his lips, as if they were clumsy pannikins* (*Great Expectations* by Charles Dickens)

pards NOUN pards are leopards ❏ *Not charioted by Bacchus and his pards* (*Ode on a Nightingale* by John Keats)

parlour boarder NOUN a pupil who lived with the family ❏ *and somebody had lately raised her from the condition of scholar to parlour boarder* (*Emma* by Jane Austen)

particular, a London PHRASE London in Victorian times and up to the 1950s was famous for having very dense fog–which was a combination of real fog and the smog of pollution from factories ❏ *This is a London particular . . . A fog, miss* (*Bleak House* by Charles Dickens)

patten NOUN pattens were wooden soles which were fixed to shoes by straps to protect the shoes in wet weather ❏ *carrying a basket like the Great Seal of England in plaited straw, a pair of pattens, a spare shawl, and an umbrella, though it was a fine bright day* (*Great Expectations* by Charles Dickens)

paviour NOUN a paviour was a labourer who worked on the street pavement ❏ *the paviour his pickaxe* (*Oliver Twist* by Charles Dickens)

peccant ADJ peccant means unhealthy ❏ *other peccant humours* (*Gulliver's Travels* by Jonathan Swift)

penetralium NOUN penetralium is a word used to describe the inner rooms of the house ❏ *and I had no desire to aggravate his impatience previous to inspecting the penetralium* (*Wuthering Heights* by Emily Brontë)

pensive ADV pensive means deep in thought or thinking seriously about something ❏ *and she was leaning pensive on a tomb-stone on her right elbow* (*The Adventures of Huckleberry Finn* by Mark Twain)

penury NOUN penury is the state of being extremely poor ❏ *Distress, if not penury, loomed in the distance* (*Tess of the D'Urbervilles* by Thomas Hardy)

perspective NOUN telescope ❏ *a pocket perspective* (*Gulliver's Travels* by Jonathan Swift)

phaeton NOUN a phaeton was an open carriage for four people ❏ *often* condescends to drive by my humble abode in her little phaeton and ponies (*Pride and Prejudice* by Jane Austen)

phantasm NOUN a phantasm is an illusion, something that is not real. It is sometimes used to mean ghost ❏ *Experience had bred no fancies in him that could raise the phantasm of appetite* (*Silas Marner* by George Eliot)

physic NOUN here physic means medicine ❏ *there I studied physic two years and seven months* (*Gulliver's Travels* by Jonathan Swift)

pinioned VERB to pinion is to hold both arms so that a person cannot move them ❏ *But the relentless Ghost pinioned him in both his arms, and forced him to observe what happened next.* (*A Christmas Carol* by Charles Dickens)

piquet NOUN piquet was a popular card game in the C18th ❏ *Mr Hurst and Mr Bingley were at piquet* (*Pride and Prejudice* by Jane Austen)

plaister NOUN a plaister is a piece of cloth on which an apothecary (or pharmacist) would spread ointment. The cloth is then applied to wounds or bruises to treat them ❏ *Then, she gave the knife a final smart wipe on the edge of the plaister, and then sawed a very thick round off the loaf: which she finally, before separating from the loaf, hewed into two halves, of which Joe got one, and I the other.* (*Great Expectations* by Charles Dickens)

plantations NOUN here plantations means colonies, which are countries controlled by a more powerful country ❏ *besides our plantations in America* (*Gulliver's Travels* by Jonathan Swift)

plastic ADJ here plastic is an old term meaning shaping or a power that was forming ❏ *A plastic power abode with me* (*The Prelude* by William Wordsworth)

players NOUN actors ❏ *of players which upon the world's stage be* (*On His Mistress* by John Donne)

plump ADV all at once, suddenly ❏ *But it took a bit of time to get it well round, the change come so uncommon plump, didn't it?* (*Great Expectations* by Charles Dickens)

plundered VERB to plunder is to rob or steal from ❏ *These crosses stand for the names of ships or towns that they sank or plundered* (*Treasure Island* by Robert Louis Stevenson)

pommel ◼ VERB to pommel someone is to hit them repeatedly with your fists ❏ *hug him round the neck, pommel his back, and kick his legs in irrepressible affection!* (*A Christmas Carol* by Charles Dickens) ◼ NOUN a pommel is the part of a saddle that rises up at the front ❏ *He had his gun across his pommel* (*The Adventures of Huckleberry Finn* by Mark Twain)

poor's rates NOUN poor's rates were property taxes which were used to support the poor ❏ *'Oh!' replied the undertaker; 'why, you know, Mr. Bumble, I pay a good deal towards the poor's rates.'* (*Oliver Twist* by Charles Dickens)

popular ADJ popular means ruled by the people, or Republican, rather than ruled by a monarch ❏ *With those of Greece compared and popular Rome* (*The Prelude* by William Wordsworth)

porringer NOUN a porringer is a small bowl ❏ *Of this festive composition each boy had one porringer, and no more* (*Oliver Twist* by Charles Dickens)

postboy NOUN a postboy was the driver of a horse-drawn carriage ❏ *He spoke to a postboy who was dozing under the gateway* (*Oliver Twist* by Charles Dickens)

post-chaise NOUN a fast carriage for two or four passengers ❏ *Looking round, he saw that it was a post-chaise, driven at great speed* (*Oliver Twist* by Charles Dickens)

postern NOUN a small gate usually at the back of a building ❏ *The little servant happening to be entering the*

CHARLES PERRAULT

fortress with two hot rolls, I passed
through the postern and crossed the
drawbridge, in her company (*Great
Expectations* by Charles Dickens)

pottle NOUN a pottle was a small basket
❑ *He had a paper-bag under each
arm and a pottle of strawberries in
one hand . . .* (*Great Expectations*
by Charles Dickens)

pounce NOUN pounce is a fine powder
used to prevent ink spreading on
untreated paper ❑ *in that grim
atmosphere of pounce and parch-
ment, red-tape, dusty wafers, ink-
jars, brief and draft paper, law
reports, writs, declarations, and bills
of costs* (*David Copperfield* by
Charles Dickens)

pox NOUN pox means sexually trans-
mitted diseases like syphilis ❑ *how
the pox in all its consequences and
denominations* (*Gulliver's Travels* by
Jonathan Swift)

prelibation NOUN prelibation means a
foretaste of or an example of something to come ❑ *A prelibation to
the mower's scythe* (*The Prelude* by
William Wordsworth)

prentice NOUN an apprentice ❑ *and
Joe, sitting on an old gun, had told
me that when I was 'prentice to him
regularly bound, we would have
such Larks there!* (*Great
Expectations* by Charles Dickens)

presently ADV immediately ❑ *I pres-
ently knew what they meant*
(*Gulliver's Travels* by Jonathan
Swift)

pumpion NOUN pumpkin ❑ *for it was
almost as large as a small pumpion*
(*Gulliver's Travels* by Jonathan
Swift)

punctual ADJ kept in one place ❑ *was
not a punctual presence, but a spirit*
(*The Prelude* by William
Wordsworth)

quadrille ■ NOUN a quadrille is a dance
invented in France which is usually
performed by four couples ❑
*However, Mr Swiveller had Miss
Sophy's hand for the first quadrille*
(country-dances being low, were
utterly proscribed) (*The Old
Curiosity Shop* by Charles Dickens)
■ NOUN quadrille was a card game
for four people ❑ *to make up her
pool of quadrille in the evening*
(*Pride and Prejudice* by Jane Austen)

quality NOUN gentry or upper-class
people ❑ *if you are with the quality*
(*The Adventures of Huckleberry
Finn* by Mark Twain)

quick parts PHRASE quick-witted ❑ *Mr
Bennet was so odd a mixture of
quick parts* (*Pride and Prejudice* by
Jane Austen)

quid NOUN a quid is something chewed
or kept in the mouth, like a piece
of tobacco ❑ *rolling his quid*
(*Treasure Island* by Robert Louis
Stevenson)

quit VERB quit means to avenge or to
make even ❑ *But Faustus's death
shall quit my infamy* (*Doctor
Faustus 4.3* by Christopher
Marlowe)

rags NOUN divisions ❑ *Nor hours, days,
months, which are the rags of time*
(*The Sun Rising* by John Donne)

raiment NOUN raiment means clothing
❑ *the mountain shook off turf and
flower, had only heath for raiment
and crag for gem* (*Jane Eyre* by
Charlotte Brontë)

rain cats and dogs PHRASE an expression meaning rain heavily. The
origin of the expression is unclear
❑ *But it'll perhaps rain cats and
dogs to-morrow* (*Silas Marner* by
George Eliot)

raised Cain PHRASE raised Cain means
caused a lot of trouble. Cain is a
character in the Bible who killed
his brother Abel ❑ *and every time
he got drunk he raised Cain around
town* (*The Adventures of
Huckleberry Finn* by Mark Twain)

rambling ADJ rambling means
confused and not very clear ❑ *my
head began to be filled very early
with rambling thoughts* (*Robinson
Crusoe* by Daniel Defoe)

raree-show NOUN a raree-show is an old term for a peep-show or a fairground entertainment ❏ *A raree-show is here, with children gathered round* (*The Prelude* by William Wordsworth)

recusants NOUN people who resisted authority ❏ *hardy recusants* (*The Prelude* by William Wordsworth)

redounding VERB eddying. An eddy is a movement in water or air which goes round and round instead of flowing in one direction ❏ *mists and steam-like fogs redounding everywhere* (*The Prelude* by William Wordsworth)

redundant ADJ here redundant means overflowing but Wordsworth also uses it to mean excessively large or too big ❏ *A tempest, a redundant energy* (*The Prelude* by William Wordsworth)

reflex NOUN reflex is a shortened version of reflexion, which is an alternative spelling of reflection ❏ *To cut across the reflex of a star* (*The Prelude* by William Wordsworth)

Reformatory NOUN a prison for young offenders/criminals ❏ *Even when I was taken to have a new suit of clothes, the tailor had orders to make them like a kind of Reformatory, and on no account to let me have the free use of my limbs.* (*Great Expectations* by Charles Dickens)

remorse NOUN pity or compassion ❏ *by that remorse* (*On His Mistress* by John Donne)

render VERB in this context render means give. ❏ *and Sarah could render no reason that would be sanctioned by the feeling of the community.* (*Silas Marner* by George Eliot)

repeater NOUN a repeater was a watch that chimed the last hour when a button was pressed–as a result it was useful in the dark ❏ *And his watch is a gold repeater, and worth a hundred pound if it's worth a penny.* (*Great Expectations* by Charles Dickens)

repugnance NOUN repugnance means a strong dislike of something or someone ❏ *overcoming a strong repugnance* (*Treasure Island* by Robert Louis Stevenson)

reverence NOUN reverence means bow. When you bow to someone, you briefly bend your body towards them as a formal way of showing them respect ❏ *made my reverence* (*Gulliver's Travels* by Jonathan Swift)

reverie NOUN a reverie is a daydream ❏ *I can guess the subject of your reverie* (*Pride and Prejudice* by Jane Austen)

revival NOUN a religious meeting held in public ❏ *well I'd ben a-running' a little temperance revival thar' bout a week* (*The Adventures of Huckleberry Finn* by Mark Twain)

revolt VERB revolt means turn back or stop your present course of action and go back to what you were doing before ❏ *Revolt, or I'll in piecemeal tear thy flesh* (*Doctor Faustus 5.1* by Christopher Marlowe)

rheumatics/rheumatism NOUN rheumatics [rheumatism] is an illness that makes your joints or muscles stiff and painful ❏ *a new cure for the rheumatics* (*Treasure Island* by Robert Louis Stevenson)

riddance NOUN riddance is usually used in the form good riddance which you say when you are pleased that something has gone or been left behind ❏ *I'd better go into the house, and die and be a riddance* (*David Copperfield* by Charles Dickens)

rimy ADJ rimy is an adjective which means covered in ice or frost ❏ *It was a rimy morning, and very damp* (*Great Expectations* by Charles Dickens)

riper ADJ riper means more mature or older ❏ *At riper years to Wittenberg he went* (*Doctor Faustus chorus* by Christopher Marlowe)

rubber NOUN a set of games in whist or backgammon ❑ *her father was sure of his rubber* (*Emma* by Jane Austen)

ruffian NOUN a ruffian is a person who behaves violently ❑ *and when the ruffian had told him* (*Treasure Island* by Robert Louis Stevenson)

sadness NOUN sadness is an old term meaning seriousness ❑ *But I prithee tell me, in good sadness* (*Doctor Faustus 2.2* by Christopher Marlowe)

sailed before the mast PHRASE this phrase meant someone who did not look like a sailor ❑ *he had none of the appearance of a man that sailed before the mast* (*Treasure Island* by Robert Louis Stevenson)

scabbard NOUN a scabbard is the covering for a sword or dagger ❑ *Girded round its middle was an antique scabbard; but no sword was in it, and the ancient sheath was eaten up with rust* (*A Christmas Carol* by Charles Dickens)

schooners NOUN A schooner is a fast, medium-sized sailing ship ❑ *if schooners, islands, and maroons* (*Treasure Island* by Robert Louis Stevenson)

science NOUN learning or knowledge ❑ *Even Science, too, at hand* (*The Prelude* by William Wordsworth)

scrouge VERB to scrouge means to squeeze or to crowd ❑ *to scrouge in and get a sight* (*The Adventures of Huckleberry Finn* by Mark Twain)

scrutore NOUN a scrutore, or escritoire, was a writing table ❑ *set me gently on my feet upon the scrutore* (*Gulliver's Travels* by Jonathan Swift)

scutcheon/escutcheon NOUN an escutcheon is a shield with a coat of arms, or the symbols of a family name, engraved on it ❑ *On the scutcheon we'll have a bend* (*The Adventures of Huckleberry Finn* by Mark Twain)

sea-dog PHRASE sea-dog is a slang term for an experienced sailor or pirate ❑ *a 'true sea-dog', and a 'real old salt,'* (*Treasure Island* by Robert Louis Stevenson)

see the lions PHRASE to see the lions was to go and see the sights of London. Originally the phrase referred to the menagerie in the Tower of London and later in Regent's Park ❑ *We will go and see the lions for an hour or two–it's something to have a fresh fellow like you to show them to, Copperfield* (*David Copperfield* by Charles Dickens)

self-conceit NOUN self-conceit is an old term which means having too high an opinion of oneself, or deceiving yourself ❑ *Till swollen with cunning, of a self-conceit* (*Doctor Faustus chorus* by Christopher Marlowe)

seneschal NOUN a steward ❑ *where a grey-headed seneschal sings a funny chorus with a funnier body of vassals* (*Oliver Twist* by Charles Dickens)

sensible ADJ if you were sensible of something you are aware or conscious of something ❑ *If my children are silly I must hope to be always sensible of it* (*Pride and Prejudice* by Jane Austen)

sessions NOUN court cases were heard at specific times of the year called sessions ❑ *He lay in prison very ill, during the whole interval between his committal for trial, and the coming round of the Sessions.* (*Great Expectations* by Charles Dickens)

shabby ADJ shabby places look old and in bad condition ❑ *a little bit of a shabby village named Pikesville* (*The Adventures of Huckleberry Finn* by Mark Twain)

shay-cart NOUN a shay-cart was a small cart drawn by one horse ❑ *'I were at the Bargemen t'other night, Pip;' whenever he subsided into affection, he called me Pip, and whenever he relapsed into politeness he called me Sir; 'when there come up in his* *shay-cart Pumblechook.'* (*Great Expectations* by Charles Dickens)

shilling NOUN a shilling is an old unit of currency. There were twenty shillings in every British pound ❑ *'Ten shillings too much,' said the gentleman in the white waistcoat.* (*Oliver Twist* by Charles Dickens)

shines NOUN tricks or games ❑ *well, it would make a cow laugh to see the shines that old idiot cut* (*The Adventures of Huckleberry Finn* by Mark Twain)

shirking VERB shirking means not doing what you are meant to be doing, or evading your duties ❑ *some of you shirking lubbers* (*Treasure Island* by Robert Louis Stevenson)

shiver my timbers PHRASE shiver my timbers is an expression which was used by sailors and pirates to express surprise ❑ *why, shiver my timbers, if I hadn't forgotten my score!* (*Treasure Island* by Robert Louis Stevenson)

shoe-roses NOUN shoe-roses were roses made from ribbons which were stuck on to shoes as decoration ❑ *the very shoe-roses for Netherfield were got by proxy* (*Pride and Prejudice* by Jane Austen)

singular ADJ singular means very great and remarkable or strange ❑ *'Singular dream,' he says* (*The Adventures of Huckleberry Finn* by Mark Twain)

sire NOUN sire is an old word which means lord or master or elder ❑ *She also defied her sire* (*Little Women* by Louisa May Alcott)

sixpence NOUN a sixpence was half of a shilling ❑ *if she had only a shilling in the world, she would be very lilkely to give away sixpence of it* (*Emma* by Jane Austen)

slavey NOUN the word slavey was used when there was only one servant in a house or boarding-house–so she had to perform all the duties of a larger staff ❑ *Two distinct knocks, sir, will produce the slavey at any*

time (*The Old Curiosity Shop* by Charles Dickens)

slender ADJ weak ❑ *In slender accents of sweet verse* (*The Prelude* by William Wordsworth)

slop-shops NOUN slop-shops were shops where cheap ready-made clothes were sold. They mainly sold clothes to sailors ❑ *Accordingly, I took the jacket off, that I might learn to do without it; and carrying it under my arm, began a tour of inspection of the various slop-shops.* (*David Copperfield* by Charles Dickens)

sluggard NOUN a lazy person ❑ *'Stand up and repeat "'Tis the voice of the sluggard,"' said the Gryphon.* (*Alice's Adventures in Wonderland* by Lewis Carroll)

smallpox NOUN smallpox is a serious infectious disease ❑ *by telling the men we had smallpox aboard* (*The Adventures of Huckleberry Finn* by Mark Twain)

smalls NOUN smalls are short trousers ❑ *It is difficult for a large-headed, small-eyed youth, of lumbering make and heavy countenance, to look dignified under any circumstances; but it is more especially so, when superadded to these personal attractions are a red nose and yellow smalls* (*Oliver Twist* by Charles Dickens)

sneeze-box NOUN a box for snuff was called a sneeze-box because sniffing snuff makes the user sneeze ❑ *To think of Jack Dawkins—lummy Jack —the Dodger—the Artful Dodger— going abroad for a common twopenny-halfpenny sneeze-box!* (*Oliver Twist* by Charles Dickens)

snorted VERB slept ❑ *Or snorted we in the Seven Sleepers' den?* (*The Good-Morrow* by John Donne)

snuff NOUN snuff is tobacco in powder form which is taken by sniffing ❑ *as he thrust his thumb and fore-finger into the proffered snuff-box of the undertaker: which was an ingenious little model of a patent* *coffin.* (*Oliver Twist* by Charles Dickens)

soliloquized VERB to soliloquize is when an actor in a play speaks to himself or herself rather than to another actor ❑ *'A new servitude! There is something in that,' I soliloquized (mentally, be it understood; I did not talk aloud)* (*Jane Eyre* by Charlotte Brontë)

sough NOUN a sough is a drain or a ditch ❑ *as you may have noticed the sough that runs from the marshes* (*Wuthering Heights* by Emily Brontë)

spirits NOUN a spirit is the nonphysical part of a person which is believed to remain alive after their death ❑ *that I might raise up spirits when I please* (*Doctor Faustus 1.5* by Christopher Marlowe)

spleen ■ NOUN here spleen means a type of sadness or depression which was thought to only affect the wealthy ❑ *yet here I could plainly discover the true seeds of spleen* (*Gulliver's Travels* by Jonathan Swift) ■ NOUN irritability and low spirits ❑ *Adieu to disappointment and spleen* (*Pride and Prejudice* by Jane Austen)

spondulicks NOUN spondulicks is a slang word which means money ❑ *not for all his spondulicks and as much more on top of it* (*The Adventures of Huckleberry Finn* by Mark Twain)

stalled of VERB to be stalled of something is to be bored with it ❑ *I'm stalled of doing naught* (*Wuthering Heights* by Emily Brontë)

stanchion NOUN a stanchion is a pole or bar that stands upright and is used as a building support ❑ *and slid down a stanchion* (*The Adventures of Huckleberry Finn* by Mark Twain)

stang NOUN stang is another word for pole which was an old measurement ❑ *These fields were intermingled with woods of half a stang* (*Gulliver's Travels* by Jonathan Swift)

starlings NOUN a starling is a wall built around the pillars that support a bridge to protect the pillars ❑ *There were states of the tide when, having been down the river, I could not get back through the eddy-chafed arches and starlings of old London Bridge* (*Great Expectations* by Charles Dickens)

startings NOUN twitching or night-time movements of the body ❑ *with midnight's startings* (*On His Mistress* by John Donne)

stomacher NOUN a panel at the front of a dress ❑ *but send her aunt the pattern of a stomacher* (*Emma* by Jane Austen)

stoop VERB swoop ❑ *Once a kite hovering over the garden made a stoop at me* (*Gulliver's Travels* by Jonathan Swift)

succedaneum NOUN a succedaneum is a substitute ❑ *But as a succedaneum* (*The Prelude* by William Wordsworth)

suet NOUN a hard animal fat used in cooking ❑ *and your jaws are too weak For anything tougher than suet* (*Alice's Adventures in Wonderland* by Lewis Carroll)

sultry ADJ sultry weather is hot and damp. Here sultry means unpleasant or risky ❑ *for it was getting pretty sultry for us* (*The Adventures of Huckleberry Finn* by Mark Twain)

summerset NOUN summerset is an old spelling of somersault. If someone does a somersault, they turn over completely in the air ❑ *I have seen him do the summerset* (*Gulliver's Travels* by Jonathan Swift)

supper NOUN supper was a light meal taken late in the evening. The main meal was dinner which was eaten at four or five in the afternoon ❑ *and the supper table was all set out* (*Emma* by Jane Austen)

surfeits VERB to surfeit in something is to have far too much of it, or to overindulge in it to an unhealthy degree ❑ *He surfeits upon cursed* necromancy (*Doctor Faustus chorus* by Christopher Marlowe)

surtout NOUN a surtout is a long close-fitting overcoat ❑ *He wore a long black surtout reaching nearly to his ankles* (*The Old Curiosity Shop* by Charles Dickens)

swath NOUN swath is the width of corn cut by a scythe ❑ *while thy hook Spares the next swath* (*Ode to Autumn* by John Keats)

sylvan ADJ sylvan means belonging to the woods ❑ *Sylvan historian* (*Ode on a Grecian Urn* by John Keats)

taction NOUN taction means touch. This means that the people had to be touched on the mouth or the ears to get their attention ❑ *without being roused by some external taction upon the organs of speech and hearing* (*Gulliver's Travels* by Jonathan Swift)

Tag and Rag and Bobtail PHRASE the riff-raff, or lower classes. Used in an insulting way ❑ *'No,' said he; 'not till it got about that there was no protection on the premises, and it come to be considered dangerous, with convicts and Tag and Rag and Bobtail going up and down.'* (*Great Expectations* by Charles Dickens)

tallow NOUN tallow is hard animal fat that is used to make candles and soap ❑ *and a lot of tallow candles* (*The Adventures of Huckleberry Finn* by Mark Twain)

tan VERB to tan means to beat or whip ❑ *and if I catch you about that school I'll tan you good* (*The Adventures of Huckleberry Finn* by Mark Twain)

tanyard NOUN the tanyard is part of a tannery, which is a place where leather is made from animal skins ❑ *hid in the old tanyard* (*The Adventures of Huckleberry Finn* by Mark Twain)

tarry ADJ tarry means the colour of tar or black ❑ *his tarry pig-tail*

(*Treasure Island* by Robert Louis Stevenson)

thereof PHRASE from there ❑ *By all desires which thereof did ensue* (*On His Mistress* by John Donne)

thick with, be PHRASE if you are 'thick with someone' you are very close, sharing secrets–it is often used to describe people who are planning something secret ❑ *Hasn't he been thick with Mr Heathcliff lately?* (*Wuthering Heights* by Emily Brontë)

thimble NOUN a thimble is a small cover used to protect the finger while sewing ❑ *The paper had been sealed in several places by a thimble* (*Treasure Island* by Robert Louis Stevenson)

thirtover ADJ thirtover is an old word which means obstinate or that someone is very determined to do want they want and can not be persuaded to do something in another way ❑ *I have been living on in a thirtover, lackadaisical way* (*Tess of the D'Urbervilles* by Thomas Hardy)

timbrel NOUN timbrel is a tambourine ❑ *What pipes and timbrels?* (*Ode on a Grecian Urn* by John Keats)

tin NOUN tin is slang for money/cash ❑ *Then the plain question is, an't it a pity that this state of things should continue, and how much better would it be for the old gentleman to hand over a reasonable amount of tin, and make it all right and comfortable* (*The Old Curiosity Shop* by Charles Dickens)

tincture NOUN a tincture is a medicine made with alcohol and a small amount of a drug ❑ *with ink composed of a cephalic tincture* (*Gulliver's Travels* by Jonathan Swift)

tithe NOUN a tithe is a tax paid to the church ❑ *and held farms which, speaking from a spiritual point of view, paid highly-desirable tithes* (*Silas Marner* by George Eliot)

towardly ADJ a towardly child is dutiful or obedient ❑ *and a towardly child* (Gulliver's Travels by Jonathan Swift)

toys NOUN trifles are things which are considered to have little importance, value, or significance ❑ *purchase my life from them bysome bracelets, glass rings, and other toys* (Gulliver's Travels by Jonathan Swift)

tract NOUN a tract is a religious pamphlet or leaflet ❑ *and Joe Harper got a hymn-book and a tract* (The Adventures of Huckleberry Finn by Mark Twain)

train-oil NOUN train-oil is oil from whale blubber ❑ *The train-oil and gunpowder were shoved out of sight in a minute* (Wuthering Heights by Emily Brontë)

tribulation NOUN tribulation means the suffering or difficulty you experience in a particular situation ❑ *Amy was learning this distinction through much tribulation* (Little Women by Louisa May Alcott)

trivet NOUN a trivet is a three-legged stand for resting a pot or kettle ❑ *a pocket-knife in his right; and a pewter pot on the trivet* (Oliver Twist by Charles Dickens)

trot line NOUN a trot line is a fishing line to which a row of smaller fishing lines are attached ❑ *when he got along I was hard at it taking up a trot line* (The Adventures of Huckleberry Finn by Mark Twain)

troth NOUN oath or pledge ❑ *I wonder, by my troth* (The Good-Morrow by John Donne)

truckle NOUN a truckle bedstead is a bed that is on wheels and can be slid under another bed to save space ❑ *It rose under my hand, and the door yielded. Looking in, I saw a lighted candle on a table, a bench, and a mattress on a truckle bedstead.* (Great Expectations by Charles Dickens)

trump NOUN a trump is a good, reliable person who can be trusted ❑ *This lad Hawkins is a trump, I perceive* (Treasure Island by Robert Louis Stevenson)

tucker NOUN a tucker is a frilly lace collar which is worn around the neck ❑ *Whereat Scrooge's niece's sister—the plump one with the lace tucker: not the one with the roses—blushed.* (A Christmas Carol by Charles Dickens)

tureen NOUN a large bowl with a lid from which soup or vegetables are served ❑ *Waiting in a hot tureen!* (Alice's Adventures in Wonderland by Lewis Carroll)

turnkey NOUN a prison officer; jailer ❑ *As we came out of the prison through the lodge, I found that the great importance of my guardian was appreciated by the turnkeys, no less than by those whom they held in charge.* (Great Expectations by Charles Dickens)

turnpike NOUN the upkeep of many roads of the time was paid for by tolls (fees) collected at posts along the road. There was a gate to prevent people travelling further along the road until the toll had been paid. ❑ *Traddles, whom I have taken up by appointment at the turnpike, presents a dazzling combination of cream colour and light blue; and both he and Mr. Dick have a general effect about them of being all gloves.* (David Copperfield by Charles Dickens)

twas PHRASE it was ❑ *twas but a dream of thee* (The Good-Morrow by John Donne)

tyrannized VERB tyrannized means bullied or forced to do things against their will ❑ *for people would soon cease coming there to be tyrannized over and put down* (Treasure Island by Robert Louis Stevenson)

'un NOUN 'un is a slang term for one– usually used to refer to a person ❑ *She's been thinking the old 'un* (David Copperfield by Charles Dickens)

undistinguished ADJ undiscriminating or incapable of making a distinction between good and bad things ❑

their undistinguished appetite to devour everything (*Gulliver's Travels* by Jonathan Swift)

use NOUN habit ❑ *Though use make you apt to kill me* (*The Flea* by John Donne)

vacant ADJ vacant usually means empty, but here Wordsworth uses it to mean carefree ❑ *To vacant musing, unreproved neglect* (*The Prelude* by William Wordsworth)

valetudinarian NOUN one too concerned with his or her own health. ❑ *for having been a valetudinarian all his life* (*Emma* by Jane Austen)

vamp VERB vamp means to walk or tramp to somewhere ❑ *Well, vamp on to Marlott, will 'ee* (*Tess of the D'Urbervilles* by Thomas Hardy)

vapours NOUN the vapours is an old term which means unpleasant and strange thoughts, which make the person feel nervous and unhappy ❑ *and my head was full of vapours* (*Robinson Crusoe* by Daniel Defoe)

vegetables NOUN here vegetables means plants ❑ *the other vegetables are in the same proportion* (*Gulliver's Travels* by Jonathan Swift)

venturesome ADJ if you are venturesome you are willing to take risks ❑ *he must be either hopelessly stupid or a venturesome fool* (*Wuthering Heights* by Emily Brontë)

verily ADV verily means really or truly ❑ *though I believe verily* (*Robinson Crusoe* by Daniel Defoe)

vicinage NOUN vicinage is an area or the residents of an area ❑ *and to his thought the whole vicinage was haunted by her.* (*Silas Marner* by George Eliot)

victuals NOUN victuals means food ❑ *grumble a little over the victuals* (*The Adventures of Huckleberry Finn* by Mark Twain)

vintage NOUN vintage in this context means wine ❑ *Oh, for a draught of*

vintage! (*Ode on a Nightingale* by John Keats)

virtual ADJ here virtual means powerful or strong ❑ *had virtual faith* (*The Prelude* by William Wordsworth)

vittles NOUN vittles is a slang word which means food ❑ *There never was such a woman for givin' away vittles and drink* (*Little Women* by Louisa May Alcott)

voided straight PHRASE voided straight is an old expression which means emptied immediately ❑ *see the rooms be voided straight* (*Doctor Faustus 4.1* by Christopher Marlowe)

wainscot NOUN wainscot is wood panel lining in a room so wainscoted means a room lined with wooden panels ❑ *in the dark wainscoted parlor* (*Silas Marner* by George Eliot)

walking the plank PHRASE walking the plank was a punishment in which a prisoner would be made to walk along a plank on the side of the ship and fall into the sea, where they would be abandoned ❑ *about hanging, and walking the plank* (*Treasure Island* by Robert Louis Stevenson)

want VERB want means to be lacking or short of ❑ *The next thing wanted was to get the picture framed* (*Emma* by Jane Austen)

wanting ADJ wanting means lacking or missing ❑ *wanting two fingers of the left hand* (*Treasure Island* by Robert Louis Stevenson)

wanting, I was not PHRASE I was not wanting means I did not fail ❑ *I was not wanting to lay a foundation of religious knowledge in his mind* (*Robinson Crusoe* by Daniel Defoe)

ward NOUN a ward is, usually, a child who has been put under the protection of the court or a guardian for his or her protection ❑ *I call the Wards in Jarndcye. They* are caged up with all the others. (*Bleak House* by Charles Dickens)

waylay VERB to waylay someone is to lie in wait for them or to intercept them ❑ *I must go up the road and waylay him* (*The Adventures of Huckleberry Finn* by Mark Twain)

weazen NOUN weazen is a slang word for throat. It actually means shrivelled ❑ *You with a uncle too! Why, I knowed you at Gargery's when you was so small a wolf that I could have took your weazen betwixt this finger and thumb and chucked you away dead* (*Great Expectations* by Charles Dickens)

wery ■ ADV very ❑ *Be wery careful o' vidders all your life* (*Pickwick Papers* by Charles Dickens) ■ *See* wibrated

wherry NOUN wherry is a small swift rowing boat for one person ❑ *It was flood tide when Daniel Quilp sat himself down in the wherry to cross to the opposite shore.* (*The Old Curiosity Shop* by Charles Dickens)

whether PREP whether means which of the two in this example ❑ *we came in full view of a great island or continent (for we knew not whether)* (*Gulliver's Travels* by Jonathan Swift)

whetstone NOUN a whetstone is a stone used to sharpen knives and other tools ❑ *I dropped pap's whetstone there too* (*The Adventures of Huckleberry Finn* by Mark Twain)

wibrated VERB in Dickens's use of the English language 'w' often replaces 'v' when he is reporting speech. So here 'wibrated' means 'vibrated'. In *Pickwick Papers* a judge asks Sam Weller (who constantly confuses the two letters) 'Do you spell it with a "v" or a "w"?' to which Weller replies 'That depends upon the taste and fancy of the speller, my Lord' ❑ *There are strings . . . in the human heart that had better not be wibrated* (*Barnaby Rudge* by Charles Dickens)

wicket NOUN a wicket is a little door in a larger entrance ❑ *Having rested here, for a minute or so, to collect a good burst of sobs and an imposing show of tears and terror, he knocked loudly at the wicket* (*Oliver Twist* by Charles Dickens)

without CONJ without means unless ❑ *You don't know about me, without you have read a book by the name of The Adventures of Tom Sawyer* (*The Adventures of Huckleberry Finn* by Mark Twain)

wittles ■ NOUN wittles is a slang word which means food ❑ *I live on broken wittles–and I sleep on the coals* (*David Copperfield* by Charles Dickens) ■ *See* wibrated

woo VERB courts or forms a proper relationship with ❑ *before it woo* (*The Flea* by John Donne)

words, to have PHRASE if you have words with someone you have a disagreement or an argument ❑ *I do not want to have words with a young thing like you.* (*Black Beauty* by Anna Sewell)

workhouse NOUN workhouses were places where the homeless were given food and a place to live in return for doing very hard work ❑ *And the Union workhouses? demanded Scrooge. Are they still in operation?* (*A Christmas Carol* by Charles Dickens)

yawl NOUN a yawl is a small boat kept on a bigger boat for short trips. Yawl is also the name for a small fishing boat ❑ *She sent out her yawl, and we went aboard* (*The Adventures of Huckleberry Finn* by Mark Twain)

yeomanry NOUN the yeomanry was a collective term for the middle classes involved in agriculture ❑ *The yeomanry are precisely the order of people with whom I feel I can have nothing to do* (*Emma* by Jane Austen)

yonder ADV yonder means over there ❑ *all in the same second we seem to hear low voices in yonder!* (*The Adventures of Huckleberry Finn* by Mark Twain)